Falling for the Wrong Brother

—

Michelle Major

HARLEQUIN® SPECIAL EDITION

Recycling programs
for this product may
not exist in your area.

ISBN-13: 978-1-335-46598-6

Falling for the Wrong Brother

Printed in U.S.A.

Michelle Major grew up in Ohio but dreamed of living in the mountains. Soon after graduating with a degree in journalism, she pointed her car west and settled in Colorado. Her life and house are filled with one great husband, two beautiful kids, a few furry pets and several well-behaved reptiles. She's grateful to have found her passion writing stories with happy endings. Michelle loves to hear from her readers at michellemajor.com.

Books by Michelle Major

Harlequin Special Edition

Crimson, Colorado

Coming Home to Crimson
Sleigh Bells in Crimson
Romancing the Wallflower
Christmas on Crimson Mountain
Always the Best Man
A Baby and a Betrothal

The Fortunes of Texas: The Rulebreakers

Her Soldier of Fortune

The Fortunes of Texas: The Secret Fortunes

A Fortune in Waiting

Harlequin Serials

Secrets of the A-List

Visit the Author Profile page
at Harlequin.com for more titles.

To Amy: thanks for being a fantastic friend and co-mom. I couldn't do it without you! XO

Chapter One

Why did wedding dresses have to be so white?

The question flitted through Maggie Spencer's mind as she hurried down the tree-lined street in Stonecreek, Oregon, the town that had been her family's home and passion for over a hundred years. Away from the First Congregational Church, away from her family and friends and from her remorseful, apologetic and cheating fiancé.

Oh, yes. Far away from Trevor Stone.

Hurried might not be the right word. It was difficult to hurry wearing five pounds of satin and lace plus high heels that pinched her feet to the point that she was ready to lop off a baby toe just to ease the pain.

She refused to take off the shoes because the physical discomfort distracted her from the ache in her chest. Tears threatened each time she thought of the repercussions of running away from her wedding five minutes before the ceremony was scheduled to begin.

The clock in the tower overlooking the town square a few blocks away began to chime, echoing the rhythmic lurch in her stomach. The wedding was starting.

Without her.

She gathered bunches of fabric in her hands and draped the dress's train over one arm. Grammy had insisted on a dress with a train, mainly so Maggie's younger sister would have a reason to hold it, putting Morgan on display for the good people of Stonecreek.

"It worked for Pippa," Grammy had commented drily. "Morgan's backside is just as worthy of going viral if you ask me."

Although no one needed to ask Grammy's opinion because she was happy to offer it unsolicited.

A car drove past, honked once. It wasn't every day that a bride took a stroll in her wedding gown. Sweat trickled between Maggie's shoulder blades, despite the June breeze fluttering the blooms on the oak trees that canopied the street. Not a cloud marred the robin's-egg-blue sky, a stroke of good luck for the marriage, according to Maggie's grandmother.

So much for positive omens.

Maggie kept her gaze forward, sending out a silent prayer the honking driver was no one she knew. Then again, most everyone Maggie knew was waiting in the church. Close to three hundred people crammed into the pews to witness the two most powerful families in Stonecreek finally united by marriage.

Or not.

She picked up the pace, wincing as her heel caught on a crack in the pavement and her ankle rolled. She'd just righted herself when a hulking SUV pulled up next to her.

"I'm fine," she called, holding up a hand and keeping her eyes trained forward as she lifted her dress higher off the ground.

"You're going the wrong way, Maggie May," a voice said, the tone a deep timbre that sent shivers along her bare arms.

The fabric dropped from her hands as that voice ricocheted through her. The tip of one heel tangled in her wedding dress, and she tripped and fell hard to the pavement. She managed to get herself to all fours, tears pricking the backs of her eyes, as much from embarrassment as the sting to her palms and knees.

She focused on drawing in a few deep breaths, but the air escaped her lungs when a pair of scuffed cowboy boots moved into her line of sight.

"Need a hand?"

"I'm fine," she repeated, giving a little shake of her head. A thousand rattlesnakes could have her surrounded and she still wouldn't accept help from Griffin Stone.

Faking composure, Maggie started to stand, then yelped when her right ankle screamed in protest.

"You're hurt." Griffin wrapped his hands around her arms and lifted her to her feet like she weighed nothing.

Glancing up through her lashes, she saw that a decade away from Stonecreek had honed him into every inch an alpha male, rugged and broad-shouldered. His dark blond hair was longer, curling at the ends as it skimmed the collar of the crisp white dress shirt he wore under a suit jacket. She knew he was well over six feet—even in her heels he towered over her. A few years older than she was, he'd been the cutest boy in high school—and the wildest by far—but now his looks were downright lethal.

"I twisted my ankle," she confirmed, shrugging out of his grasp and trying not to put weight on her right leg. "Stupid shoes. I still don't need your help." She glared at him. "What are you doing here anyway? Trevor said you weren't coming back for the wedding, and you never RSVP'd."

He inclined his head and she felt more than saw his smile, a slight softening around the corners of his stormy green eyes. "Last-minute change of plans."

"You're late," she muttered, sweat beading on her forehead as the pain in her ankle began to radiate up her leg. She needed to get away from Griffin and take off the stupid heels her bridesmaids had convinced her to buy.

"Apparently, I'm not the only one." He took a step forward, then reached around her to open the passenger-side door on his vintage Land Cruiser. "You don't have to like me, Maggie, but get in the car before you pass out from the pain of whatever you did to your ankle."

She bit down on her lip to keep the tears at bay. Of all the people to see her in this state, why did it have to be Griffin? He'd been the star of every one of her foolish teenage fantasies. She hadn't even cared that bad-boy Griffin Stone barely acknowledged her existence, even though she and Trevor had been friends since she'd thrown up on him their first day of kindergarten.

Griffin was three years older and a world apart from Maggie. He'd made it clear in the sneering, searing way he had that he thought her nothing more than a silly, spoiled princess. Now she was a pathetic mess.

It grated on her nerves to have Griffin bear witness to the most humiliating moment of her life. Chances were good he'd eventually congratulate his younger brother for escaping a lifetime shackled to the darling of the Spencer family. That thought was equally irritating since her only sin had been trusting the wrong man.

She gingerly put her right foot on the ground, hoping the pain might have miraculously disappeared. Instead, a sharp stab of pain caused her to whimper, and she turned without a word and hobbled the few steps to the Land Cruiser.

To his credit, Griffin didn't say anything or try to help her. It was like he could sense that her composure was as thin as an eggshell and might splinter into a thousand pieces if he got too close. She hated feeling fragile, hated being hurt, hated Trevor and his litany of excuses.

Griffin shut the door when she finally managed to get herself up into the SUV and gather the dusty fabric of her wedding gown's train into the vehicle.

He'd left the Land Cruiser running, and Maggie was profoundly grateful for the cool air blowing from the vents. The strap of the heel cut into her flesh, but she didn't pull off the shoe. There was a decent chance she'd scream or throw up if she did, and neither was going to happen in front of Griffin.

"I'm guessing we aren't headed back to the church," he said as he pulled away from the curb.

"I bought Grammy's house a few years ago. She lived—"

"I know where your grandmother lived." Griffin's knuckles turned white gripping the steering wheel. "I grew up here."

She had the odd sense she'd hurt his feelings, although that would be far-fetched on a good day. Griffin had always made his derision for Stonecreek crystal clear, and he'd left them all behind the first chance he got. Still, she couldn't help being a champion for the town. It was in her blood. "The neighborhood has a lot of young families now. It's nice."

Griffin's response was a noncommittal grunt, and Maggie let out a sigh. She shouldn't be trying for small talk, not under the best of circumstances, and let alone when she was running away from her wedding to his younger brother.

Trevor had promised he'd stall as long as possible, so Maggie figured she had about thirty minutes until her family descended on the two-story Cape Cod–style house she'd purchased from her grandmother three years ago.

Grammy wasn't going to take the news well, no matter how justified Maggie was in walking away.

Another complication, because Maggie couldn't tell her grandmother the truth. She'd promised Trevor—

"What did he do?" Griffin asked suddenly, like he could read her mind.

"It wasn't Trevor." The words were sawdust in Maggie's throat. "He'll always be a friend, but we were never suited for marriage." She gave what she hoped was a bittersweet smile. "I'm just sorry it took me so long to realize it."

That was good. She sounded regretful but not angry. Surely, people would accept her explanation. Everyone knew Maggie Spencer wouldn't lie.

"Is he gay?" Griffin asked conversationally.

Maggie's eyes widened. "No. We had a healthy… I mean, we're both busy so it wasn't exactly… Just no."

"Another woman? A gambling addiction? Internet porn?"

"Why can't you believe I made the choice to walk away?"

"Because you always do what's expected, and a union between the Spencers and the Stones is something people around here have wanted for ages." He pulled up in front of her house and threw the Land Cruiser into Park. "You don't have the guts to defy them."

Too stunned to move as Griffin got out of the SUV, Maggie watched him walk around the front toward her side. It was like he'd clocked her with a sledgehammer. A man she hadn't seen for almost a decade—a man who'd never said a nice thing to her in all the years they'd known each other—had just summed up her life in one sentence, and it didn't reflect well on her.

Especially because it was true.

"You don't know me," she said through clenched teeth as he opened the door. She went to push past him, a challenge with her ankle, but it didn't matter. Griffin scooped her into his arms, ignoring her protests, and stalked toward the front door.

"Is it locked?"

"No," she muttered, "and put me down."

"Once we're inside."

He shifted his hold to reach for the doorknob, pulling her more tightly against his chest. She couldn't help but breathe in the scent of him, tempting and dark like every rebellious thought she'd ever had but never acted on.

His heat enveloped her and she fisted her hands in the lapels of his navy suit jacket. She had the unbidden urge to press her mouth to the suntanned skin of his throat and forced her gaze to remain fixed on his striped tie.

The house was quiet, and he set her gently on the sofa, then knelt down in front of her.

"What are you doing?"

"Checking your ankle." He pushed up the fabric of her gown, revealing her open-toe sandals with the delicate pearl detail across the straps. The shoes were elegant and glamorous and she needed them off her feet about as much as she needed to breathe.

Yet Griffin touching her was too much when she was in pain and emotionally vulnerable.

"I can handle it."

"Let me look." He undid the ankle strap, and she was amazed at how gentle his calloused hands were as they gripped her leg. "I was a combat medic during my time in the army."

The pain had lessened slightly, or maybe she'd become numb to it. "You wore your dress blues to your dad's funeral." It was the last time Griffin had been home to Stonecreek, although she doubted he considered the town his home any longer.

His broad shoulders stiffened, but he nodded.

"Are you out of the army now?"

Another slight nod.

She winced as he manipulated her ankle, rotating it gently to one side then the other. "Why did you leave?"

He glanced up at her, his gaze both guarded and intense. "Why didn't you marry my brother?"

"I already tol—"

"Trevor did something, Maggie." He lowered her foot to the floor and sat back as he studied her. "Tell me what it was."

"So you can rush off and slay my dragons?" she asked with a laugh, flipping her gown down over her knees. "Playing the part of hero doesn't suit you, Griffin."

Something flashed in his gaze, but it was gone before she could name it. "An understatement, especially coming from you." He stood and rubbed a hand across the back of his neck. "Your ankle should be fine when the swelling goes down, but you might want to rethink your heel height in the future."

She bent forward and undid the strap on her other shoe. "It was my wedding day. The shoes were special."

"It's a strange phenomenon," he said quietly, "the focus on the details surrounding a wedding. Seems to me the only important part is a man and woman committed to loving each other for the rest of their lives."

Emotion clogged her throat. "Yes, well… Trevor and I love each other. We've been friends forever. Everyone knows it."

Griffin raised a thick brow. "Then what are you doing here?"

A car door slammed, saving her from answering.

"My family," she whispered, glancing around wildly like she could find a place to hide. A ridiculous idea, because there was no hiding from what she'd done today. Not in Stonecreek.

"I'll go out the back, then circle around to get my car." Griffin was already moving toward the hallway leading to the kitchen. "No one is going to want me here for this."

I do, Maggie wanted to tell him, although she couldn't figure out why. Griffin was nothing to her.

"Are you staying in town long?" she blurted, using the arm of the sofa to lever herself to standing. She needed to be on her own two feet—or at least the one that wasn't screaming in pain—to face her grandmother.

Griffin looked over his shoulder, raking a hand through his already-tousled hair. The air between them sparked, his gaze going dark as Maggie sucked in a breath.

"Put some ice on that ankle," he said instead of answering, then disappeared down the hall.

A moment later the front door burst open and various members of her family flooded through.

"Are you okay?" her father asked, tugging at his black bow tie.

"Are you crazy?" Vivian Spencer, Maggie's grandmother, asked, pushing past her son. "You can't call off the wedding, Mary Margaret. It isn't done."

"She just did." Maggie's sister, Morgan, followed Grammy into the house, picked up a cardboard box from a wingback chair and then sat down.

"No sass from you," Vivian scolded, wagging a finger at Morgan.

Sixteen-year-old Morgan, the picture of teenage petulance, responded with an eye roll and a dismissive sigh. Grammy's eyes narrowed, although her angry gaze returned to Maggie.

"I'm sorry," Maggie said, looking at each of her family members.

Her fourteen-year-old brother, Ben, shrugged out of his rented tux jacket. "You should have seen how bad people were freaking out," he told her, his eyes going wide. "Trevor's mom looked like she wanted to shank someone."

"Definitely me," Maggie muttered.

"Jana Stone wasn't going to shank anyone," their father said. "Naturally, she's upset and confused." He glanced toward Maggie and then away. "We all are."

Ben didn't look convinced. "If someone handed her a rusty knife, she would have gutted Maggie like—"

"Not helping, Ben." Jim Spencer leveled a glare at his teenage son.

Undeterred by the gruesome talk, Vivian moved toward Maggie until they were inches apart. Grammy barely reached Maggie's chin and she'd proudly been a size-two petite for as long as anyone could remember. Her hair was teased into a silver pouf, and she wore a rose-hued coat and matching crepe dress that made her look like she took fashion advice from the Queen of England.

Her diminutive stature belied the fierceness of her spirit. Maggie's grandmother was more than the family matriarch. She was the backbone of the Spencer clan, still with a hand in actively managing most of the family's business holdings in town and the land they owned throughout the valley.

The Spencers, along with the Stones, had founded Stonecreek in the mid-1800s. It still grated on the nerves of various relatives, Grammy included, that the town had officially been named Stonecreek instead of the planned Spencerville.

The Stones claimed that founders Jonathan Spencer and Charles Stone flipped a coin for naming rights. According to Spencer family lore, Charles got Jonathan drunk, then sneaked out to file the town's name in the early-morning hours while his friend slept off a night of whiskey and women.

That spark lit the fuse on the Hatfield-and-McCoy-esque rivalry between the two families. The friction had ebbed and flowed over the decades until settling into a civil, if awkward, truce.

Recently, the animosity had heated up again. The Spencers had been the more successful family for years, owning most of the businesses in town, as well as much of the land in the surrounding area. But Griffin and Trevor's father took over the struggling family farm when the boys were still in diapers. Dave Stone began growing grapes in the volcanic soil and within a decade had turned the vineyard into one of the leading producers of pinot noir varietals in the lush Willamette Valley.

Suddenly, power shifted, and the rural farming family began to assert its muscle in ways the Spencers didn't appreciate. The power play was subtler these days, with deals over dinner and drinks more than fistfights at town meetings. It had been Vivian who'd pushed Maggie to view Trevor as something more than a platonic friend.

Both of them had gone away to college, then returned to Stonecreek to work with their respective families. It had been easy to ramp up the childhood friendship to a more intimate level.

They'd dated for three years, and Trevor had been at her side when she'd won her first mayoral election, becoming the youngest person to hold that office in the town's history.

If you asked her grandmother, it was the two families' combined support that had propelled Maggie, relatively inexperienced in politics, to victory in the election. But Trevor had made her feel like she'd won on her own merit, and remained quite possibly the only person in either of their families who believed it.

He'd proposed last Christmas. Of course, Maggie had said yes. So what if their relationship was more of a comfortable partnership than romantic or exciting? She didn't need excitement and believed Trevor felt the same. Oh, how wrong she'd been.

"You embarrassed me today," her grandmother said, pale blue eyes flaring with temper, "and brought shame to the Spencer name."

Maggie swallowed and purposely put weight on her right foot, focusing on the physical pain instead of the emotional sting of her grammy's words.

"Mom." Maggie's father let out an exasperated sigh. "Let her explain."

"Can you explain yourself, Mary Margaret?"

"I changed my mind," she whispered, her gaze trained on the corsage pinned just below the collar of her grandmother's dress. "Trevor and I realized we don't love each other in the way two people who are getting married should." She couldn't look Grammy in the eye as the half-truths spilled from her mouth.

Not complete lies. She went into the wedding with a bone-deep understanding that her marriage to Trevor had more to do with her family than any kind of grand passion. But she would have gone through with it if she hadn't walked in on him locked in a furtive embrace with the curvaceous date of one of his groomsmen.

"What did Trevor do?" Grammy demanded, much

like Griffin had earlier. Good thing Maggie wasn't a gambler because she clearly had no poker face.

"Nothing." She lied outright this time. She'd decided at the church that she'd rather be the bad guy in this scenario than the poor, duped and undesired fool. Trevor had agreed. He would have agreed to anything Maggie had asked. "I'm sorry, Grammy. I'll take back the gifts and write apology notes to each of the guests. I'll do whatever it takes to make this right."

Vivian held up a weathered hand, the manicured tips of her fingers trembling. "This cannot be undone, Mary Margaret." She turned to Maggie's father. "Take me home, Jim."

He glanced between his mother and older daughter. "Maybe Maggie doesn't want to be alone right—"

"She made her choice," Vivian said through clenched teeth. She waved a hand at both Morgan and Ben. "Let's go."

Morgan stood and placed a hand on her dad's sleeve. "I can stay with—"

"We're all going," Vivian insisted, walking toward the front door without a backward glance.

"It's fine," Maggie whispered when Morgan's delicate brows drew together. "I'll text you later, Mo."

Her father took a step toward her, but Maggie shook her head. "It's okay. Go. I'm fine."

He looked like he wanted to argue, but she forced a smile and motioned for him to follow Grammy. Right now she needed time alone.

"I love you," her dad whispered, then walked out behind Grammy and Morgan. Ben turned back to her with his hand on the doorknob.

"I wouldn't have let Mrs. Stone shank you," he said gravely.

Maggie managed a watery smile. "Thanks, buddy."

He nodded, shutting the door behind him. As soon as the latch clicked, Maggie's knees buckled. She collapsed to the hardwood floor with a sob, her life in pieces around her.

Chapter Two

Griffin pushed open the church doors and strode through, ignoring the gasps and stares of the small crowd still gathered near the front of the sanctuary.

His younger brother stood in the center aisle between the pews, talking to a woman Griffin didn't recognize, although she seemed vaguely familiar.

Growing up it felt like Griffin had known everyone in the close-knit community, and he'd chafed at both the expectations and scrutiny of being part of one of Stonecreek's founding families. How could he expect anonymity when the town bore his family's damn name?

He hadn't asked for any of it. Small-town life had been stifling enough to a rambunctious kid without the added pressure of trying to live up to what his parents wanted from him. It had been presumed he'd be groomed to take over the helm of the family vineyard. Everyone in town—except his father—had seen his future like it had already come to pass.

Griffin knew Dave Stone would never have allowed him to take over the business. Griffin hadn't been able to please his demanding father, and by the time he'd hit his troubled teen years, he'd stopped trying. Let Trevor be lauded as the family's favored child. Griffin had always been more suited to the role of black sheep.

He watched as Trevor smiled and inclined his head as the older woman patted his shoulder, playing the part of the brokenhearted groom to a T. If he hadn't been set on becoming the family scion, Trevor could have had a career in Hollywood. This little performance showed he was a consummate actor, although Griffin didn't believe a moment of it.

People turned as he stalked up the aisle, but his full attention was on Trevor. He hadn't seen his brother since their father's funeral four years ago. Trevor was a couple of inches shorter than Griffin, his hair a shade lighter, making him look even more the golden son.

"Griffin." Trevor's deep voice boomed through the nearly empty sanctuary. He opened his arms, preparing to greet the prodigal brother with a hug. As if that would ever happen. "Good to see you, man. Sorry you came all this way for—"

Griffin slammed his fist into Trevor's face without a second thought, the sharp pain in his knuckles a welcome outlet for his frustration.

Trevor muttered a curse as he stumbled back a few steps, covering his left eye with one hand. "What the hell was that for?"

"You tell me." Griffin shook out his hand, then

turned to meet the shocked gazes of the people still standing in the back of the church. "If you folks will excuse us, my brother and I need to speak in private."

"Maggie left him," said the older woman, whom Griffin finally recognized as his high school health teacher. "She walked out just as the ceremony was starting. It wasn't his fault. Trevor's the victim here. His poor face."

"Victim," Griffin repeated. "I don't think so."

"You don't know anything," Trevor said, the skin around his eye already turning a satisfying shade of purple.

"Really?" Griffin crossed his arms and arched a brow, letting Trevor know without words that he wasn't fooled by the jilted-groom act. "Do you want to have this conversation here or in private? Think long and hard about your answer, Trev."

Griffin was bluffing. Maggie had told him nothing, but he couldn't shake his suspicion that she'd had more of a reason for playing the runaway bride than she'd let on. Walking away wasn't in her character, and he didn't buy his self-important brother as the jilted groom for one minute.

Trevor stared at him for a moment, his eyes unreadable. Then a muscle ticked in his jaw, and Griffin wanted to punch him again. He recognized Trevor's tell from when they were kids, and Griffin knew without a doubt his brother was guilty of something.

"I'm not going to bore these nice people with our family drama," Trevor said, his tone smooth like Harvest Vineyards' flagship pinot.

"It's not boring," the health teacher—Mrs. Davis if Trevor remembered correctly—said enthusiastically.

Trevor flashed the most charming smile he could with his swollen eye. "You're a sweetheart, Mrs. D, and I'd appreciate a few of your famous oatmeal scotchies the next time you bake a batch. Right now, I'm going to take a minute with my brother." He glanced around the church, as pious as a choirboy. "This isn't the place for violence."

Immediately, Griffin regretted letting his temper get the best of him. Or at least he regretted hitting Trevor in a church. His mother would have a fit when she heard about it, and he'd already caused Jana Stone enough trouble to last a lifetime.

"I'll talk to you all soon," Trevor called to the rest of the onlookers. "Thanks for the support today."

Griffin looked over his shoulder as he followed Trevor toward the vestry. The few people who'd witnessed his outburst were whispering among themselves and met his gaze with a round of angry glares. Only an hour back in Stonecreek and he was bristling to escape again.

He didn't bother closing the door as Trevor walked to a small refrigerator positioned in the corner of the room and pulled a bottle of water from it.

"Did you talk to Maggie?" he asked, wincing as he pressed the water bottle to his eye.

"Yes. I was late for the ceremony and saw her walking down the sidewalk."

"I'm surprised you recognized her."

"She was wearing a damn bridal gown."

Trevor sighed. "I told her she could take my car when she left."

"A gentleman to the end," Griffin muttered, pacing to one side of the room and running a hand along the edge of the bookshelf lined with hymnals.

"What did she tell you?"

Griffin forced himself not to stiffen. "I want to hear it from you."

"Maggie promised she wouldn't talk. She said she understood." Trevor blew out a frustrated breath. "Neither one of us meant for it to happen. I tried to cut things off. Hell, she was here with Tommy. He was one of my groomsmen. I introduced them four months ago. You remember him, right?"

"The fool who accidentally set himself on fire at homecoming your freshman year?"

"The bonfire after the football game got out of hand," Trevor said almost reluctantly. "He's grown up a lot since then. Sort of."

"So you set your mistress up with an idiot? Nice backup plan."

"I chose Maggie," Trevor insisted. "But if she won't forgive—"

"She didn't tell me anything," he said through clenched teeth.

Trevor's mouth fell open. "Then how did you—"

"I didn't," Griffin interrupted. "Not until this moment. Maggie's version was that she realized the two of you were better as friends and she couldn't go through with the marriage."

"It's the truth," Trevor said, dropping into a chair positioned next to a rack of black robes.

This cramped room wasn't quite the pulpit, but Griffin still felt a stab of guilt for his violent thoughts under the church roof. "Not the whole truth."

"Hell, Grif, I tried. We both did. This wedding meant more to the families—more to the town—than to either of us."

"What a lame excuse for cheating."

Trevor's mouth tightened into a thin line. "I wasn't cheating today. Not really."

"Then what did Maggie see?"

"Julia and I were kissing. A farewell kiss."

"In the church before your wedding ceremony?" Griffin laughed without humor. "You're going to act holier-than-thou because I punched you in the sanctuary? The angels were probably cheering me on."

"What do you care?" Trevor demanded. "You told me you weren't even going to be here today. Suddenly you feel the need to come to Maggie's defense? You never liked her when we were younger. You have no relationship with her. I don't get it."

Griffin turned away toward the window overlooking the glen behind the church. The towering maple trees provided a lush green canopy, and tulips in a variety of colors lined the cobblestone path. Lilac bushes bloomed with lavender flowers, a short burst of color that would be gone by summer.

He'd spent most of the past decade in war-torn countries across the Middle East. Places baked by the sun, where it was as common to breathe in sand as air. There'd been moments where he'd felt like his throat would always be coated with the stuff, and he'd closed his eyes late at night and imagined himself back in this verdant valley.

He'd foregone college and joined the army against his parents' wishes. Life in Stonecreek had felt like it was choking him after a stupid mistake fractured any possible relationship with his father. It wasn't until he'd traveled halfway around the world that he'd realized how much home meant to him.

He hadn't wanted to come back here. Too many demons from his past lurked in the shadows. It seemed like he'd never be able to shrug off the disappointment and failure that were part of who he was in this town.

Trevor was the living embodiment of that. Three years younger, his brother had a knack for causing trouble but not being caught up in it. It was like Trevor wore a coat of armor preventing people from seeing anything but the best in him. The polar opposite of Griffin.

He might not have a relationship with Maggie, but the connection he felt had been immediate and almost palpable. He'd seen her walking down the street in that fancy gown, and his heart stuttered. How had the annoying, gangly girl he'd grown up with morphed into such a beautiful—and achingly melancholy—woman?

Every one of his boyhood transgressions had been magnified by the insinuation that he made his family look bad in front of the upstanding Spencers. Maggie had been their goody-two-shoes princess. The fact that she and Trevor had been friends despite the animosity between the two families hadn't surprised Griffin. They'd both been textbook perfect. But today she'd seemed truly alone. Griffin had always been a sucker for another loner.

"She doesn't mean anything to me," he lied. "I felt sorry for her, and obviously with good reason."

"You don't need to feel sorry for Maggie. She's tougher than she looks."

"That doesn't make it right."

"It wasn't my fault."

It never is, Griffin thought to himself.

"Do you love this Julia?" he asked.

Trevor pressed his fingers to his eyelids as if the

question gave him a headache. "Not exactly, but I can tell you I never felt anything like it with Maggie."

Griffin snorted. "Two years ago I ate some bad scallops in Dubai, and I've never felt anything like what came next."

"Shut up, Grif."

"You can't let Maggie take the fall for—"

"You're back!"

Both men turned as Jana Stone raced into the room. She spread her arms wide and Griffin walked into his mother's embrace, his heart swelling as she pulled him close. At five feet two inches tall, his mother barely grazed his chest, but a hug from her made him feel like he was a kid again.

He'd lost count of the times he'd been sent to his room by his father for one transgression or another. His mother had always sneaked upstairs to give him a hug and reassure him of his father's love.

He'd even spent one full Christmas dinner alone, sulking on his bed, after he'd accidentally knocked over the tree while he and Trevor were wrestling. The fight had started when Trevor purposely broke a radio-controlled robot Griffin had unwrapped earlier, but it didn't matter to his dad.

Griffin was the older brother who should have known better, so he'd been the one punished. When his mom couldn't convince Dave Stone to give him a break because of the holiday, she'd boycotted the family meal, making up two plates and joining him in his room.

They'd eaten cross-legged on the floor, taking turns choosing Christmas carols to sing. It had been one of the best Christmases Griffin could remember, free of the tension and awkward silences that accompanied regular family dinners at the vineyard.

"Why didn't you tell me you were coming?" she asked, giving him another squeeze before pulling away. She sucked in a breath as she glanced toward Trevor. "Oh, my gosh. What happened to your eye?"

Trevor helpfully pointed at Griffin, who yelped as his mother pinched him hard on the back of the arm.

"You hit your brother? What were you thinking?" She placed a hand on her chest. "Tell me you didn't fight with your brother in church."

"Can't do that, Mom. Sorry."

"You should be sorry, Griffin John Stone. After all Trevor has been through today. I swear I wouldn't put it past Vivian Spencer to have orchestrated this whole fiasco just to embarrass our family."

"I highly doubt it," Griffin muttered.

"Maggie had to follow her heart," Trevor said, sounding like the benevolent son his mother knew him to be. "No one is to blame."

"*She* is to blame," their mother countered. "You're the vice president of marketing for Harvest Vineyards. You're a public figure, Trevor. We did a special blend for the occasion." She threw up her hands. "With personalized labels. Press releases went out. This could hurt the brand."

"Mom." Griffin shook his head. "This was supposed to be a wedding, not a publicity event."

He glanced at his brother, who lifted his brows as if to say *I told you so.*

"You've been away from Stonecreek too long, Griffin. Social media has blurred the lines between our private lives and public branding for the company. There's too much competition these days to think otherwise."

She moved toward Trevor, gently touching the swelling around his eye. "We certainly have no time for nonsense between the two of you. I guarantee the Spencers are already doing damage control. What do you think this will do to Maggie's prospects for reelection in the fall?"

"Nothing," Trevor said immediately. "She's done a great job as mayor this first term so there's no reason to think she won't win again."

Jana tsk-tsked softly. "She won the first time because we endorsed her—she had the support of the whole town." She straightened and turned to Griffin. "Your second cousin is running against her. He's been giving me the 'blood is thicker' line for months. Everyone has seen that Mary Margaret Spencer can't follow through on a commitment of the most important kind. How can they trust her running Stonecreek? Especially given the Spencer single-mindedness in promoting a civic agenda benefiting her family's business interests."

Griffin rubbed the back of his neck. He'd returned because his mother had asked him to, but he didn't want any part of this small-town drama. "Hasn't the animosity between the two families gone on long enough?"

"We thought so," Jana admitted. "I know Jim wants peace between us. I do, too." She worried the pad of her thumb back and forth over the ring finger on her left hand, where she'd worn her wedding band for over two decades until her husband's death. "Today changed everything."

"Do you have something to add to this conversation?" Griffin asked Trevor.

His brother only shook his head and whispered, "Not now."

"Fine. I'll do it." Griffin turned toward his mother. "There are things about today you don't understand. Like the reason I hit Trevor."

The bejeweled purse hanging at her side began to buzz incessantly. "It's your grandmother," Jana said, pulling out the phone. "I'm late to pick her up. She's going to help me take the flowers from the reception site. We need to get to them before Vivian does. They'll work for a tasting event at the vineyard tomorrow night, but you can bet Vivian Spencer will use them for the inn if given half a chance."

"Mom, we need to talk."

"Later tonight," Jana promised, already heading for the door. "Family dinner at the house." She glanced toward Griffin. "Did you drop your stuff there already?"

"Not yet."

"I cleared out the caretaker's apartment above the garage like you asked, although I don't know why you won't move back into your old room. It's far more convenient." She blew each of them a kiss. "No fighting, you two. I mean it."

"Moving back?" Trevor asked as soon as she was gone. "To Stonecreek?"

"It's only for a few months," Griffin said, examining a scratch on one knuckle. "While I build the new tasting room."

"Wait a minute." Trevor stood and held up a hand. "You're the contractor Mom hired?"

Griffin nodded. "I asked her not to mention it to you."

"No way. You don't get to waltz back in here and start taking over. I've dedicated the past five years to the family business."

"I'm not a threat to you," Griffin said quietly. "I know my place."

"Since when?"

Griffin ignored the verbal jab. "I also know my way around a construction site and have a sense of the history of the vineyard. Mom wants it to be right, and I owe it to her."

"I'm the vice president—"

"Of marketing," Griffin interrupted.

Trevor narrowed his eyes. It was no secret his dream in life was to run Harvest Vineyards. Both of them had grown up working the land and learning the ins and outs of the wine-making process. As Griffin grew older, the animosity between him and his father had grown until the two hundred acres they owned felt like a cage, the home he'd lived in since he was born, a prison.

"Dad wouldn't have wanted this," Trevor said harshly. "After what you did…"

"Not his decision to make any longer."

Their father had died four years ago when the private plane he'd chartered crashed just after takeoff. The accident had been a shock to them all, and a huge blow to their mother. But Jana took her role as president of the board as seriously as if she'd been born into the family.

Griffin had come back for the funeral and stayed for the family meeting his mother insisted on presiding over the morning after the service. He knew Trevor had expected to be named CEO but instead Jana had offered the position to their longtime employee, Marcus Sanchez.

"I still should have been told."

"And you still need to tell Mom about why Maggie walked away," Griffin countered, unwilling to debate his worthiness to return to the vineyard with his younger brother.

Trevor studied him for a long moment, then flashed a sanctimonious grin. "You won't stick, Grif. You never do."

Fists tightly clenched, Griffin watched his brother walk out of the room. How could he argue when the desire to climb into his SUV and drive away made his skin itch like a junkie looking for his next fix?

He wasn't meant for Stonecreek. He'd been a different person here, a punk kid he didn't like very much. But he also had no idea how to be anyone else when faced with his past.

So where did that leave him?

He sure as hell wished he knew.

Chapter Three

"Do you hate me?"

Maggie paused in the act of folding the last of the tablecloths that would have been used at her reception. It was nearly eleven at night, and the Miriam Inn's ballroom was dark other than one dim bulb glowing in the entry, where Brenna Apria stood, her arms wrapped tightly around herself.

"Does it matter?" Maggie asked, then placed the tablecloth on top of the pile with more force than necessary. Nancy Schulman, who managed events at the inn, had called her earlier to report that Trevor's mom and grandma had descended on the venue and were scooping up the vases of flowers that Maggie and her bridesmaids had arranged and placed around the room the previous day.

The Spencers owned the inn and event center, and

Maggie had recommended Nancy for the manager position after a nasty divorce nine months ago. Maggie appreciated that the woman still felt some loyalty, when Grammy had made it clear in a barrage of texts and voice mails throughout the day that everyone else thought Maggie was either crazy or downright cruel to have left poor, sweet, upstanding Trevor Stone at the altar.

Maggie hated to admit how much it hurt that people who'd known her since she was in diapers could turn on her so quickly, but she wouldn't let it show. That was something she'd learned from her mother, who'd put on a brave front even when ovarian cancer ravaged her, metastasizing throughout her body.

She'd told Nancy to let the Stone women take whatever they wanted and that she'd clean up the rest after. Then she'd called the florist, the DJ and the photographer to personally apologize and assure them she'd pay each of their bills in full.

Even knowing they were getting their money, none of the vendors had been happy. Working the Spencer-Stone wedding was more than a regular job. The two families were practically royalty in the growing town, and Harvest Vineyards was quickly gaining a national reputation for its wine.

But the loss of visibility and free marketing couldn't be helped. At least not by Maggie. It was rapidly dawning on her exactly what she'd done with her promise to Trevor about keeping the real reason she'd walked away a secret.

Now the woman she'd considered her best friend, who'd known about Trevor's cheating, was standing here looking for what? Forgiveness? Absolution?

Maggie was fresh out of both.

"It matters. You're my best friend." Brenna walked forward, in and out of shadows, but Maggie could see how miserable she looked. Her dark eyes were red, her high cheekbones stained with the tracks of dried tears. Maggie didn't care. Her own face was puffy from crying and even now, when she thought she had no more tears to shed, she could feel moisture prick the corners of her eyes.

She bit down on the inside of her cheek until she tasted blood. "How long have you known?"

"Trevor promised he'd change," Brenna insisted instead of answering the question, then broke off at the glare Maggie sent her. "That it was a onetime lapse in judgment. I wanted to believe him, and I didn't want you to be hurt."

"That backfired," Maggie muttered.

"You have no idea how sorry I am."

"You're supposed to be my best friend."

"I am," Brenna whispered.

Maggie grabbed the tablecloths and shoved them into a cardboard box. "You were aware my fiancé was cheating and didn't tell me. I caught him swapping spit with another woman minutes before the wedding, and you weren't even shocked. Did you know about Julia?"

Brenna's full lips pressed into a thin line. "I thought it had ended, but they were flirty at your engagement party. I asked Trevor about it, and he said I was overreacting. He told me I'd ruin both of your lives if I said anything."

"Don't you think it would have been worse if I'd ended up married to a cheater?"

"He told me—"

"You must know you have terrible judgment when it comes to men," Maggie said through clenched teeth, unable to stop herself, even though she knew the comment was hurtful.

Brenna grimaced. "I know." She picked up a stack of napkins and thrust them toward Maggie. "You can hit me if you want, like Griffin did with Trevor. I deserve it as much as him."

Maggie stilled as unease snaked along her spine. She hadn't admitted anything to Griffin, so it was difficult to imagine him defending her to his brother. And yet... "What do you mean Griffin hit Trevor?"

"Decked him in front of the pulpit. Mrs. Davis was standing just a few feet away. She said Griffin looked like he wanted to kill Trevor but only threw one punch. Apparently, Trevor has a nasty shiner."

"Have you seen him?"

Brenna shook her head. "I also didn't realize Griffin was back in town. I thought he said he wasn't coming to the wedding."

"He had a change of plans," Maggie told her.

"You talked to him?" Brenna's brows shot up.

"As I was leaving the church," Maggie said with a nod. "He ended up giving me a ride home."

Brenna's sharp intake of breath was audible in the quiet space. "What does he know?"

Maggie bristled at the implied accusation in her friend's—former friend's—tone. "Nothing he heard from me. Trevor was the one who betrayed me, Brenna. I understand that, but it doesn't change how hurt I am that you didn't tell me what you knew."

She walked to the far side of the reception hall, where they'd set up a table for the buffet line. Thankfully, after a few hours off her feet with an HGTV-watching marathon, her ankle felt almost normal again so she wouldn't have to recount her embarrassing fall to Brenna. At one end of the long table stood a framed photo of Maggie and Trevor—their official engagement photo.

It had been taken just after Christmas, the two of them standing together on the bridge that spanned the creek snaking through the park in the middle of town. Snow covered the trees and their cheeks were rosy from the cold air. They looked happy. She'd *been* happy, or so she thought.

"I don't know why I agreed to take the blame for canceling the wedding in the first place." She lifted the picture off the table, gripping the frame so tight her knuckles went white. "How is it better this way?"

"It shows people that you were in control," Brenna suggested weakly.

"They hate me."

"No one could ever hate you," Brenna countered but they both knew that wasn't true.

"Why, Brenna?" Maggie hated the catch in her voice. "Why not talk to me? If I'd known, I would have broken up with him months ago."

Brenna put up her hands, palms out, defending herself from Maggie's simple line of questions. "I believe he loved you, and you deserve happiness more than anyone I know. I'd never do anything to hurt you. At least tell me you believe that."

"I do," Maggie agreed reluctantly. She and Brenna had met soon after Maggie returned to town when they'd taken a yoga class together. It was an unlikely friendship—Maggie had just been elected mayor and

Brenna had just filed a restraining order against her latest ex-boyfriend. "Can I ask you a question?"

Brenna nodded. "Of course."

Maggie appreciated both the other woman's commitment to making her life better and the fact that she didn't seem to care about Maggie's angelic reputation or who her family was in town. Brenna had been the first person since Maggie graduated college and returned to Stonecreek who liked Maggie for herself.

Brenna had a six-year-old daughter, Ellie, whom Maggie adored, and the two women had become fast friends. So much that when Jana Stone needed to hire a new assistant to work in the family's office and manage the vineyard's tiny tasting room, Maggie had recommended Brenna for the job.

She hadn't had a moment's doubt about her fiancé and where Brenna's loyalty would lie if it came to that. On paper, Maggie and Trevor were perfect, and she'd been willing to ignore the rather flat chemistry and lack of spark in favor of all the practical things they had in common. She'd assumed he felt the same. What an idiot she'd been.

"Do you think…" She paused, looking for the right words. When none came she simply blurted, "Was Trevor that desperate to not marry me?"

"Maggie, don't go there." Brenna wrung her hands in front of her waist. She'd changed from her bridesmaid's dress into a pair of black yoga pants and a baggy sweatshirt but other than her blotchy face, she was still a knockout. A few inches taller than Maggie's five-foot-six-inch frame, Brenna had curves for days. Combined with her olive skin and thick caramel-colored hair, men noticed her wherever she went.

"I need to know. Was he using the affair to force me to walk away so he didn't have to?"

"I believe so."

The simple statement was a physical blow. It was bad enough to believe that Trevor had betrayed her because he'd found his soul mate in another woman, but hearing that he just couldn't stand the thought of marrying Maggie? It was too much.

"You don't think they're in love?"

Brenna shook her head, a strand of shiny hair escaping the elastic band at the back of her hair.

"He should have told me he didn't want to go through with it." Maggie pressed her fingers to her temples. If she really examined the last couple of months, she could see the cracks in her relationship with Trevor turning into gaping chasms. They hadn't been intimate since…well, far too long. He'd shown no interest in wedding plans, which she'd attributed to him being a man and nothing more.

"I'm sorry I didn't say anything," Brenna repeated, and her voice cracked. "I don't want to lose you."

Maggie sighed. She didn't want to end the friendship, despite Brenna's dishonesty. Trevor was the one to blame in all this. She'd never admit it out loud, but the more she thought about a life without him at her side, the more relief spilled through her.

Had she really gotten so caught up in planning a wedding that she ignored the fact she didn't want to marry the man whose ring she wore? What did that say about her and how much she'd allowed her life to be dictated by what her family and the town expected of her?

"I'll call you next week," she offered, because the breach of trust still stung.

"Okay," Brenna agreed, swiping at her cheeks. "If you need anything…"

"Time," Maggie said quietly. "I need time."

"You deserve better than him," Brenna whispered, then turned and left Maggie alone in the empty reception hall once again.

"You're also too nice," a deep voice said from the back of the hall. "I remember that now."

She turned to see Griffin emerging from the door that led to the kitchen area.

Annoyance pricked Maggie's spine at the subtle condemnation in his words. As if being nice was a bad thing. "She apologized, and your brother's the one who cheated. What would you have me do?"

"Tell her she's a sorry excuse for a friend," Griffin suggested. "Yell and scream at her for not having your back."

Maggie grabbed another pile of napkins and shoved them into the box. "Or give her a black eye like you did to Trevor?"

One side of Griffin's mouth hitched up as he examined the knuckles on one hand. "It felt good."

"I told you I don't need you to defend me. Walking away from the wedding was my choice." She stalked forward, maneuvering around tables until she stood toe-to-toe with him. "What are you doing here anyway? Do you have some new sixth sense for predicting my lowest moments so you can watch and gloat?" She couldn't conceal the anger in her tone. Maggie always kept a tight hold on her emotions, but with Griffin she seemed unable to hide anything.

"Mom sent me over to pick up the cases of wine."

She stilled as he reached out a finger and traced it along the curve of her cheek. The touch was feather-light, and she resisted the urge to lean into it. Maggie had lived every day of her life surrounded by family, friends and the town she loved...until today. Now she was alone, and the solitude chafed at her in a way that made her feel weak. She hated being weak.

"Brenna was right about one thing," Griffin told her. "My brother doesn't deserve you, and he sure as hell doesn't deserve your tears."

"It's *my* canceled wedding," Maggie said, making her voice light. "And I'll cry if I want to."

Griffin's green eyes softened, but he dropped his hand as if he realized the moment was too intimate. "What next?"

"Back to life." Maggie stepped away. "We weren't scheduled to leave on the honeymoon for a few weeks, so Monday it's business as usual at city hall."

"Right." Griffin gave a slight nod. "You're Stone-creek's incumbent mayor."

The thought of facing everyone at work and the members of the town council made a sick pit open in Maggie's gut. "When do you take off?"

Griffin didn't answer, so Maggie turned back to him, holding the cardboard box in front of her like a shield. He watched her, his gaze unreadable. "What?"

One broad shoulder lifted and lowered. "I may not be leaving for a while."

She concentrated on breathing, feeling like a thousand-pound weight sat on her chest. "How long is a while?"

Another shrug. "My mom wants me to build the

new tasting room at the vineyard, and I've tentatively agreed. I owe her since the fire in the original building was my fault."

"It was a stupid accident. Everyone knew that."

A muscle ticked in his jaw. "I think Dad never rebuilt because he wanted the reminder of how badly I'd failed him. Mom claims it's important someone in the family oversees the project. We still need to work out the particulars, but I might be around a few months."

"Oh." Her lips formed the word as her brain scrambled for purchase. Griffin Stone back in town. It shouldn't matter. It shouldn't affect her, not after everything that had happened today. But it did, and her reaction to him made all the other chaos in her life lose focus.

The only thing she could see was the tall, handsome man who'd come to her defense—even when she'd told him not to—standing in front of her.

"I'm going to start loading the wine," he said, still studying her. "See you around, Maggie."

She gave a small wave, then continued packing up boxes, telling herself Griffin didn't matter to her.

Too bad her heart refused to be convinced.

Chapter Four

Monday morning Griffin stood on the hilltop that overlooked the estate vineyard, emotion pinching his chest as he breathed in the musky scent of earth. The rows of vines spread across the property, neat and orderly like soldiers in a procession.

As a kid he'd spent hours running through the fields, measuring the progress of the seasons by the height of the vines and the colors of the grapes. The vineyard below him was called Inception, the first Dave Stone planted when he'd converted the farm, which had been marginally successful at best, to a vineyard.

Griffin had loved everything about the land until it became clear that his father didn't think him worthy to be involved in the family business. It had never made sense to Griffin. He was the older son, and he felt a connection to the vines in his heart, unlike Trevor, who'd been more interested in the flashy side of wine making only—the marketing and brand positioning.

But his dad had ever only found fault with the innovations and ideas Griffin suggested. Even the way Griffin hand harvested the grapes was never right. Eventually he'd stopped trying, at least when his father was around. He'd watch the workers during the harvest, pretending he was too interested in his own life to care about the vineyard.

It had always been a lie.

"Jana told me she'd convinced you to return," a voice said from behind him. "I wasn't sure I believed her."

Griffin turned as Marcus Sanchez, Harvest Vineyards' current CEO, walked up from the direction of the main office.

He held out a hand and Marcus shook it with a surprising amount of enthusiasm. "It's good to have you back."

"Only temporarily," Griffin clarified.

Marcus inclined his head. He was nearing fifty but still had the build of a younger man, with broad shoulders and a thick crop of dark hair. "You've been away from home too long, Grif. You belong on this land."

Griffin swallowed and kicked at a patch of dirt. Strange how much those words meant to him after all this time. Marcus had worked at Harvest for almost fifteen years, so he'd had a front-row seat to Griffin's teenage battles with Dave Stone.

Although he worked for Dave, Marcus had always been kind to Griffin, unlike many of the employees who seemed to feel like part of their loyalty to Dave included shunning Griffin. "Mom says she'd be lost without you around here. Thanks for taking care of her."

Marcus flashed a grin. "Your mother can take care of herself, and we both know it."

"I'm surprised she was able to lure you away from the grapes." He inclined his head toward Marcus's pressed jeans and dress shirt. "You clean up nice."

"Jana is a difficult woman to refuse." Marcus adjusted his collar with tentative fingers as if he was still unused to having his shirts starched. He'd come to work as a picker and quickly risen through the ranks until being promoted to vineyard manager a decade earlier.

"Tell me about it." Along with most everyone associated with Harvest, Griffin had expected Trevor to be made CEO after their father's death. Instead, Jana convinced Marcus to move from the fields into the corner office.

"Have you visited the winery yet?" Marcus asked.

Griffin shook his head. "I walked the fields but haven't made it inside yet. The expansion looks great."

"We took cuttings from the original vines to plant the newest vineyard. Your mother named it Promise." Marcus nodded. "The entire operation is certified sustainable now, and we've started bottling with eco-friendly glass and managed to eliminate some of the high-risk chemicals that were originally used for fertilization and in the pesticides."

"How's that going?" Griffin felt himself clench his hands into fists.

"It's making Harvest more responsible and adding to the efficiency of the operation. Just like you told your dad years ago."

Griffin blew out a breath. "I'm sure the technology has come a long way since then."

"It was still your idea," Marcus said softly. "And a good one."

"Thanks." The tension coiling through Griffin eased slightly. The argument about protecting the long-term health of the land had been one of the last he'd had with his father before their final, irrevocable falling-out.

Griffin had been a senior in high school and planning to go to college to study viticulture. Back then he'd still believed if he could prove to his father that he could offer value to the business that Dave Stone would find a place for him. But his dad had brushed aside the suggestions, asserting that it was too soon to worry about the future when they were still trying to establish the brand.

"There's more to be done," Marcus suggested quietly.

"You mean besides rebuilding the tasting room?" Griffin massaged a hand against the back of his neck. "Mom told me about her plans for a restaurant and guest cottages on the property."

Marcus shook his head. "I'm talking about additional sustainability measures. Making Harvest Vineyards not just a steward of the land but a true innovator in the industry. You could help."

"Not me. I'm here for the construction project and nothing more."

"You know this land and you have a sense of the business."

"Maybe I did back in the day, but not anymore. I work with my hands."

"That's what wine making is." Marcus held out his weathered hands, turning them over to expose the calluses on his palms.

Griffin chuckled. "You haven't gone soft yet."

"I spend time in the fields whenever I can." Marcus lifted a heavy brow. "I could do more if I had someone to take over the business end."

"You have Trevor."

"I'm not talking about designing labels and schmoozing distributors."

"You can't deny it's part of the industry."

"Your brother is immensely talented, but he doesn't see the big picture of the legacy of what your dad started here. He never did, Grif."

"But Dad wanted him, not me." Griffin pressed his lips together, hating the bitterness in his tone. He was a grown man. You'd think he'd be over not being his daddy's favorite by now. But it was more than that.

Marcus bent forward, plucked a blade of grass from the hillside and twirled it between his fingers. "You're a lot like your father."

"You don't have to say that." Griffin shook his head. "Hell, I don't want to be anything like him…except…"

He didn't need to finish the thought. Marcus knew. In a moment of weakness when Griffin was seventeen, after a blowout with his dad, he'd escaped to the fields and found Marcus carefully pruning a row of vines. He'd admitted out loud his biggest fear in life—that Dave Stone was not his biological father.

Neither of his parents had ever given him any indication that was the truth, although it would explain so much about his tense relationship with his dad. Griffin knew his parents' courtship had been a whirlwind and although he'd never had the guts to ask his mom outright, he'd often wondered if there had been someone else before his dad.

"He was your father," Marcus said. "Don't doubt it. You got all your bullheadedness from him."

"It doesn't matter now," Griffin said, even though they both knew it did. "You've done a great job around here. You don't need my help." He turned to survey the area where the new building was set to be constructed. "I've gone over the plans from the architect. There are a few things I'd like to tweak, but it's a solid design."

"We still need to get approval from the town council's development committee."

Griffin nodded. He'd worked with enough building departments over the past couple of years to understand what hoops they'd need to jump through.

"Everyone knows the fire was an accident." Marcus opened his fingers and the blade of grass fluttered to the ground. The words were a direct echo of what Maggie had told him.

"Dad didn't," Griffin muttered, repeating his stock answer. "I still can't believe he never rebuilt the tasting room. Using the lobby of the office for all these years makes Harvest Vineyards look like an amateur operation. Visitors expect an experience when they tour a winery, not being shoved into a cramped room."

Marcus sighed. "Your dad was too stubborn for his own good. We can thank Trevor for pushing the idea of building a new tasting room. It's part of his overall branding strategy."

"My brother's not stupid," Griffin said. Then he added, "At least when it comes to the business. His personal life is another story."

"I thought Maggie called off the wedding?"

"Let's just say she had more reason than just cold feet."

Marcus groaned. "Then Trevor's a fool. He isn't going to find a better woman than Maggie Spencer."

"Agreed." Griffin pressed three fingers to his chest where it tightened at the thought of seeing Maggie again. He had no business with her, and it was stupid to go anywhere near her for a dozen reasons, not the least of which was the canceled wedding. But erring on the side of caution was never his strong suit.

"I've got a conference call in a few minutes with one of our distributors." Marcus glanced at his watch. "Let me know if there's anything you need to move things along with construction. And when you're ready for more, my office is open to you."

Griffin huffed out a laugh. "You're like a dog with a bone," he muttered.

Marcus smiled. "Whatever it takes."

Brenna practically jumped out of her chair when the door to the main office opened. She breathed a sigh of relief as Marcus Sanchez walked through. Marcus was not quite six feet tall, with the lean frame of a man who'd spent most of his life working the fields.

She knew he missed the vines now that he was in the office most days. He favored pressed jeans or khakis with tailored shirts but had extras hanging in the hall closet since he often returned to the office after lunch with dirt stains on his shirts.

Whether clean or rumpled, Marcus had the air of a man who tolerated nothing less than perfection, which made him all the more intimidating to Brenna. She knew she was outwardly pretty but her inside was a jumble of insecurity and downright fear. Fear that she'd disappoint her daughter. Fear that she'd mess up her life more than she already had. Fear that she'd never find the happiness she so desperately craved.

"Are you okay?" His gentle brown eyes searched her face like he could read her innermost thoughts.

Terrified at the idea, Brenna pasted on a bright smile and tapped a finger on the edge of the computer monitor. "You startled me, that's all. I'm working on the schedule for the rest of the month. Trevor sent an email adding a few events." She pressed her lips together, forcing herself to stop babbling to Marcus.

The vineyard's serious CEO didn't need Brenna blathering on about her duties. But she was so worried about a possible confrontation with Trevor that adrenaline spiked through her, making her stomach jittery and her nerves strung tight.

Marcus gave her a warm smile. "How much coffee have you had this morning?"

"Oh, my gosh." Brenna popped out of her chair, banging her knee on the corner of the desk in the process. "I'm sorry. I forgot to make a fresh pot," she said, turning and hurrying down the hall toward the small kitchenette that was the company's break room.

She made coffee every morning, often pairing it with homemade muffins or sweet bread. Her official title was office assistant, but for the past six months she'd also managed the makeshift tasting room set up on one side of the Harvest Vineyards lobby.

Trevor had been the one to promote her into that position, and she was grateful for the additional responsibility and bump in pay. They didn't get a ton of tourist traffic like some of the larger vineyards, although the plan was for that to change with the opening of the new tasting room. But Brenna made sure the visitors who did find them got not only samples of their best vintages but also a warm welcome to the area.

Most of her work was with Trevor or the winery's operations manager. Although he was the CEO, Marcus liked to schedule meetings and handle personal correspondence himself. She tried not to take it personally but secretly wondered if he didn't ask for her assistance because he didn't trust her to do a good job.

Now she wished she had the tall, handsome leader in her corner. She hadn't spoken to Trevor since Maggie had walked out of the church. But he must know Brenna had been the one to confirm that the kiss was more than a onetime lapse in judgment. Why hadn't she told Maggie about his cheating before?

She'd betrayed her best friend and herself. Brenna had made plenty of mistakes, but she'd promised herself to be stronger in character when she moved to Stonecreek. Her six-year-old daughter, Ellie, was depending on her. It was the reason Brenna hadn't gone on one date since the move. She wanted to be a role model for her girl, not a cautionary tale like her own mother had been. Somehow, she'd still managed to mess things up.

She yanked the empty coffeepot off the counter and turned on the tap to refill it, startling again when a hand touched her shoulder.

"Something's wrong, Brenna," Marcus said quietly.

She wanted to scream. Or cry. Or run away. Maybe all three at the same time would do the trick. Other than superficial office pleasantries, she and Marcus had barely spoken in the year she'd worked at Harvest. She wasn't even sure he knew her name until this moment. Okay, Harvest employed fewer than a couple dozen people full-time, so of course Marcus knew her name. He saw her every day of the workweek.

He'd just never said it before. Hearing it and the sincerity in his tone almost undid her. She felt dirty and cheap in a way she hadn't even when her last boyfriend had put his hands on her in violence. She'd thought Trevor was her friend and had trusted him when he'd told her he loved Maggie.

Trusting the wrong people had always been her downfall. If only she'd had a Marcus in her life— someone constant and caring. Someone who might see her as something more than a pretty face.

"I'm a horrible person," she blurted, pouring the water into the coffee maker with shaking fingers. Anything to keep moving so she wouldn't break down completely.

"You're not," he countered.

She shoved the pot under the dispenser, flipped a lever and then whirled on him, unable to accept kindness she most definitely didn't deserve.

"Trevor was cheating on Maggie, and I knew it." She crossed her arms over her chest like she could ward off the judgment she was sure to see in Marcus's dark eyes. "I caught him with a woman months ago, but I never said anything to Maggie. She's my best friend and I didn't tell her."

Marcus's gaze was unreadable, his features a mask that was almost as disconcerting as outright condemnation. "Why?"

She opened her mouth, then shut it again. "Does it matter?"

"To me it does."

"He told me he loved her and was sorry," she whispered. "I wanted to believe him, and maybe he meant it. But Maggie is the best friend I've ever had. I betrayed her by not saying anything." She threw up her hands. "She even got me the interview with Jana for this job."

"I know."

"I love this job."

One side of his mouth quirked. "I know."

"I thought Trevor was a good guy. I thought he was my friend."

A muscle ticked in his jaw. "The two of you were certainly friendly—huddled around the computer or laughing together serving wine to guests."

She shook her head automatically. "No. It wasn't like that. I didn't mean for it to be taken that way. I'm flirty with men. It's my thing." She pointed a finger at him. "I hope you aren't insinuating that I did anything inappropriate with Trevor. I'm sure he's angry that I confirmed with Maggie that I knew he'd cheated. I could lose my job because of it, but I won't let you slut-shame me."

He took a step back, held up his hands, palms up, color rising to his cheeks. "Whoa there. I don't think you're a slut and I'm not shaming you for anything. You don't flirt with me," he added. "I'm a man."

"You're different."

"How?"

"You're the boss."

He let out a huff of a laugh. "Really?"

"I respect you," she said after a moment. "I want you to take me seriously."

"I do respect you," he told her. "You aren't going to lose your job because of this."

"If Trevor—"

He hitched a thumb at his chest. "Remember—I'm the boss."

"What about Jana?"

"She can deal with her son and his actions. I'll keep you safe, Brenna."

The air whooshed out of her lungs at the simple statement. That was the thing missing from any relationship she'd ever had with a man—the feeling of safety. She had a self-destructive streak a mile long. Marcus's words felt like a promise, and she tucked them into her heart.

He only said it because he was a nice guy. It didn't mean anything. She couldn't let it mean anything. She'd been fooled too many times to let her heart open to a man like Marcus Sanchez. He was way out of her league.

"I won't mess up like that again." She smoothed a hand over the floral-patterned dress she wore, fingering one of the delicate buttons. "This job is too important."

He gave a slight nod and moved forward. For a moment she thought he was going to reach for her. And in that moment, she wanted it. Wanted to be held by a man who valued her, to know what that felt like for once in her life.

"I'll make the coffee today," he said, his voice gruffer than normal. As if on cue, she heard the distant sound of the chime over the office's main entrance. "You'd better go see who's here."

"Thank you," she whispered and hurried out of the room. She might not be the sharpest knife in the drawer, but Brenna knew enough to accept a second chance.

Chapter Five

"You can't avoid the world forever. It's cowardly and not how a Spencer behaves."

Maggie stifled a groan as her grandmother barged into her office on the third floor of the historic building that housed Stonecreek's courthouse, city hall and police department.

"I'm working, Grammy." She stood, coming around the edge of the desk to give Vivian the requisite hug and kiss on her cheek. "The Pioneer Day Festival is next weekend. I've been updating the website and putting together last-minute posts for social media."

Maggie was Stonecreek's only full-time administrative staff member, so she took on most of the responsibilities for promoting the town—as well as dealing with city council, permits and contracts, plus anything else the community needed from her.

"You should be out in the community," Grammy

insisted, wagging a finger in Maggie's direction, "not hiding behind your computer."

"This is part of my job, too," Maggie argued. "It's not hiding."

Grammy tsk-tsked, then gripped Maggie's arms. "You have to show them you're not embarrassed by your horrible mistake and total lack of judgment."

"When you put it like that..."

"People are angry, Mary Margaret, and rightfully so. Your wedding was supposed to be the event of the year."

A sick pit opened in the center of Maggie's stomach. "Do you want to see the summer calendar? We have a half dozen great events scheduled. One of them can take the place of my wedding."

"They pale in comparison to your wedding," Vivian countered. "You're royalty in this town. The Spencers have always represented what's best about Stonecreek. Then Dave Stone had to open his winery and slowly that family has been chipping away at our status with their fancy wines. The Stones were nothing but a bunch of dirt-poor farmers before Harvest Vineyards."

"Grammy," Maggie said with a sigh, "we've talked about this before. The vineyard is good for the town. It brings in more tourism dollars. People come for the wine but they stay to discover everything else we have to offer."

"But the vineyard is the lure now. That isn't how it used to be. It isn't how we *want* it to be." Vivian stepped away, her lips pursed. "We want them here for the antiques and the tearoom. We need them to stay at our inn, Maggie, not stop through as part of a valley wine tour. We're losing control, and that's unacceptable."

Maggie hated to see her grandmother so upset. The Spencers had owned the majority of the businesses in downtown Stonecreek for most of the town's history. There was the Miriam Inn and Tearoom, named for Maggie's great-great-grandmother, and the Stonecreek Antiques Market across the street.

Her family also owned the market on the corner, which had been managed by a neighbor for the past twenty years. Maggie's uncle Frank ran the Stonecreek Realty and Property Management Company, making him the landlord for most of the other businesses in downtown. A small faction of residents, led by members of the Stone family, lamented the fact that the Spencers held a bit of a monopoly in town.

Truth be told, Harvest Vineyards leveled the playing field and tilted the balance of power in a way that Maggie's family had never before seen. Secretly, she thought it was about time but she'd never admit that out loud. To do so would be tantamount to a betrayal of her family's legacy.

"We can still work with the Stones," she said, trying another tack. "Trevor and I breaking up doesn't change that we all want what's best for Stonecreek. I'm going to put together a proposal for Jana Stone and Marcus Sanchez to detail some ideas I have for cross promotions that will benefit both the town *and* Harvest."

"It isn't the same as being connected by marriage," Grammy insisted, although her tone had gentled slightly. "They have no reason for loyalty to us now. Dave Stone carried a chip on his shoulder for most of his life that the Spencers were more successful than his family."

"Jana isn't Dave. Neither is Trevor."

"She's a mother whose son was humiliated in front of her friends and family. If you don't think Jana and Trevor are going to want to exact some kind of revenge, you're being naive."

Maggie bristled at her grandmother's words. If anyone had a right to feel humiliated, it was her. Trevor was a genius at marketing, his work propelling Harvest wines to the national spotlight, critical acclaim and an ever-growing client base.

She couldn't help but think the timing of the kiss with Julia hadn't been an accident on his part, especially after talking to Brenna. Her friend thought Trevor had used the other woman to get out of the marriage. How did Trevor really feel at this point?

"I'll make things right with the Stones," Maggie promised. "Trevor and I were friends long before anything romantic happened between us. He'll make sure his mom knows that in the end it was for the best."

"And you'll stop hiding?" Vivian prompted.

Maggie nodded, although her throat went dry at the thought of venturing outside the safety of her office. "I was about to break for lunch," she said brightly. "Care to join me?" If Vivian came, Maggie could use her grandmother like a shield. No one would dare mess with her if her petite but stalwart Grammy was at her side.

"No, thank you, dear." Vivian approached Maggie again and patted her cheek. "Go to The Kitchen. It's the best place to be seen on a weekday afternoon."

"Because Irma Cole is the biggest gossip around," Maggie muttered.

"Play nice, Mary Margaret. I'm depending on you. Summer will pass quickly, and Election Day will be here before you know it. We can't let Jason Stone gain any traction."

After dropping a quick kiss on the tip of Maggie's nose, Vivian turned and walked out of the office, leaving a trail of White Diamonds–scented air in her wake.

Hands numb and palms sweating, Maggie went back to her computer and saved the graphic for the Pioneer Day Festival. Stupid to think she could go back to normal without facing the events of last weekend. Maybe it wouldn't be so bad, she told herself as she grabbed her purse, then left her office.

She slipped into the hall and gave a little wave to Megan Roe, the young woman who served as the secretary for Maggie, as well as police dispatcher and administrative support for the fire department. Megan, who was as eternally optimistic as her boss, smiled brightly and put her thumb in the air. "You've got this," she said with a nod.

Maggie had relied on Megan over the past couple of days to bring in food and coffee while Maggie was holed up in her office. She'd gotten to work before daybreak and stayed until the town was dark, skulking through the sidewalks like she had something to hide.

She didn't, but no one else knew that and she hadn't been ready to face censure from a community that believed she'd failed it.

Maggie got out of the building without seeing anyone else—maybe because she'd hurried to the back staircase and out the door that opened to the alley behind city hall. Heart hammering in her chest, she made her way through the shadowed walkway between two buildings. She stopped before reaching the main sidewalk and forced a few deep breaths.

This was the plight of being a good girl, Maggie thought to herself. Twenty-seven years old and she didn't know how to deal with disappointing the people around her. She'd been the kid who did chores without being asked and made her bed each morning. She'd been the teacher's pet in every grade, even more so in high school after her mother died. The structure and routine of school was the only thing that kept her sane when her father was falling apart in the months after cancer claimed his wife's life.

Her grandmother had stepped in, but with her dad so out of it and her mom no longer around to run interference, Maggie had been on the receiving end of the brunt of Vivian's attention.

Maggie wanted to make sure Morgan and Ben had normal childhoods—or as normal as kids could have without a mother. So she'd feigned interest in the lectures her grandmother constantly spouted on Spencer pride and expectations.

Maybe it was an inevitable osmosis, but eventually Maggie had gained a deep appreciation for her family's identity in town and taken up the mantle of the Spencer legacy. It had given her a purpose she'd desperately needed at that point.

Now that purpose was coming back to bite her in the butt. She paused at the corner of the building as her eye caught on a sign stuck into the soft ground at the edge of the park across from city hall.

There were two signs, actually. One advertised the

upcoming pancake breakfast, an annual fund-raiser held to raise money for the parks committee that she oversaw as part of her mayoral duties. Beneath that was another, hand-painted poster with the words Meet Candidate Jason Stone. Loyal. Dependable. He Won't Waffle.

She lifted her hand to the cool brick to steady herself. It was starting already. The repercussions of her decision on Saturday. Grammy had warned her people would use it against her. One mistake that wasn't even really a mistake, but she was still going to pay a price.

"Pancakes and waffles. He's going with a breakfast slogan." Maggie startled as Griffin moved into the shadows between the two buildings, the heat of his body making the air in the cool shade rise several degrees. "I prefer eggs and bacon, if you were wondering."

"It's not fair," she whispered, her gaze straying back to the sign.

"Don't tell me you're one of those 'I skip meals because I'm on a diet' women," he said, shaking his head. "Or worse, that you only have smoothies in the morning."

She blinked, turned to face the man at her side. He wore an olive green T-shirt, frayed at the collar, and faded jeans with a baseball cap on his head. "What are you talking about?"

"Breakfast." He said the word like it was obvious. "I told you my penchant for protein and you answered, 'It's not fair.'"

She scrunched up her nose, trying to follow his meandering train of thought. "I wasn't talking about food." She pointed to the sign across the street. "I meant it's not fair that Jason can use the fact that I canceled the wedding as part of his campaign."

Griffin tapped his chin as if he was just catching on to her meaning. "The waffling thing?"

"Yes," she said through clenched teeth. "The waffling thing."

"That guy has rocks for brains, obviously. It's been that way since we were kids. My nana barely acknowledged his part of the family, but Trevor and I used to have a great time baiting him at random family functions when we were together. We could tell him anything and he'd believe it. He's got the IQ of a caveman."

"Once again," Maggie said, holding up a hand, "I'm going to ask. What are you talking about?"

"Waffling," Griffin explained. "Not the breakfast food this time. He's not using the word right. To waffle you would have to walk away from Trevor, then change your mind and try to get back together with him. *To waffle* is to not be able to make up your mind. That wasn't what happened." One thick brow rose. "Unless you're thinking of reuniting?"

"Of course not."

"Then there's no waffling." He leaned in closer and she could smell the clean scent of shampoo and soap. Her stomach dipped. "Have you ever done it before?"

"I-it?" she stammered, her mind racing in a thousand inappropriate directions.

His lips curved like he knew exactly what she was thinking. "Walked away from a wedding," he clarified.

"No."

"Then you can't even be considered a serial runaway bride." He flashed a wide grin. "Get it? *Serial* versus *cereal*. I'm sticking with the breakfast analogies."

Maggie groaned but her chest no longer felt like an anvil was weighing it down. "Enough," she said, stifling a laugh. "What are you doing here?"

He glanced around the shadowed walkway. "I was heading to the hardware store and saw you in a dark alley. I thought you might need rescuing from a pickpocket or potential mayor-napper or something along those lines."

Maggie frowned.

"*Rescuing* is the wrong word." He held up his hands. "Backup. I thought you could use backup."

Once again Griffin had found her in a moment of need and was managing to make her feel better. His hair curled around the edges of his ball cap, and there was a layer of stubble shadowing his jaw like he hadn't bothered to shave this morning. Trevor had always been immaculately smooth shaven, to the point where Maggie wondered if he was one of those guys who drove around with an electric razor in his glove compartment.

Not Griffin. Griffin probably didn't care what anyone thought of him. Or what anyone thought of her, for that matter.

"I was going to get lunch," she said. Then she added on in a rush of breath, "Want to come?"

He studied her for a moment, scratching his jaw. How could that sound be so sexy? Then he leaned out from the shadows, glancing toward the front of city hall. "Why are you sneaking out the back door?" he asked, his gaze returning to her. "Did you need to stow your cape in the alley before hitting the light of day?"

She snorted. "I'm the antihero around here these days."

"You shouldn't be relegated to shadows, Maggie May. You've done nothing wrong."

The knot around her heart began to tighten again, and she raised fingers to her chest like she could manage her breathing that way. "Last Saturday was this town's version of a royal wedding, and I ruined it."

"Trevor—"

"I'm not heartbroken," she interrupted. "I'm embarrassed and angry but not heartbroken. People are going to see it in my face. I'm not even sure I really wanted to marry your brother, and part of me is relieved I had an excuse to walk away. That makes me the biggest coward on the planet." She threw out a hand toward the park across the street. "I'm worse than a waffler or a serial heartbreaker. I'm a big fat chicken."

"That's not breakfast," he said with a smile, "but you can serve it with waffles, so I'll let it slide."

She huffed out another laugh. "Do you take anything seriously?"

"Too much," he admitted quietly and while she couldn't name the emotion that darkened his green eyes for a fleeting moment, she felt it all the way to her toes. "Let's go have lunch, Maggie. If this town wants something to talk about, we'll give it to them."

She bit down on her lip and nodded, unable to form words at the moment without breaking down completely. With Griffin at her side, she stepped out into the bright sunshine of the perfect June afternoon.

Chapter Six

Griffin and Maggie were on the receiving end of several nasty stares as they walked a block to the restaurant. The Kitchen was obviously as popular now as it had been when he was a kid, based on the crowd milling about on the sidewalk.

A gaggle of women openly pointed and whispered until Maggie lifted a jaunty hand and called out a greeting. He was so damn proud of her in that moment, even though he could see her fingers shaking as she lowered her arm and clutched it to her side.

"Is my brother that popular in town these days? I can't figure out why everyone cares about your wedding."

The tip of her tongue darted out to wet her upper lip, sending a shocking jolt of awareness through him. This was the third version of Maggie he'd seen since returning to Stonecreek, this one different than either the perfectly coiffed runaway bride or the dejected, deflated woman cleaning up at the reception hall late at night.

Today she wore what he imagined amounted to her version of a power suit—a tailored skirt and matching jacket in a pale shade of blue with a white scoop-neck T-shirt underneath. Her hair was pulled back into an understated ponytail. Her makeup—if she wore any— was subtle. Maybe a coat of mascara highlighting her gray eyes and a bit of lip gloss, but he could see the freckles that dotted her nose and cheeks. He liked her better like this than fancy as she'd been on her wedding day. She even smelled different, more like fresh shampoo and less like expensive perfume.

She was more the Maggie he remembered but still changed from the girl he'd once known. Her gaze was unsure and her shoulders hunched ever so slightly.

His gut had twisted when he'd seen her cowering in the shadowed alley. All the color drained from her face as she stared at the campaign sign his idiot relative had strategically placed across the street from city hall. Jason wasn't book smart, but he clearly still had a mean streak a mile long.

Griffin should have walked away, turned around and gotten back in the Land Cruiser. He'd come into town to talk to Kurt Meyer, who owned the town's hardware store and lumber supply company. There was a big-box store about forty minutes up the road, but Griffin was determined to use local vendors as much as he could for the project at the vineyard. Instead, he'd walked right past the hardware store and crossed the street to town hall, inserting himself into business that didn't concern him in the least.

"It's not exactly about Trevor," she said, turning to him just before they got to the restaurant. "It's bigger than that. You know what our two families mean to this town."

"The nonwedding doesn't change anything."

"Are you sure?" Her throat moved as she swallowed. "The truce between the Spencers and the Stones has been tenuous at best. A lot of people around here remember a time when the families' fighting spelled disaster for the rest of the town."

"That was the past. Nothing like that would happen now."

Maggie picked an invisible piece of lint from her sleeve. "The wedding cost the vineyard both publicity and wine—all those bottles specially labeled for the occasion. You've been gone a long time. Things have changed. Stonecreek relies on support from the vineyard. Your family backs the hospital foundation, the school district, and a grant from Harvest almost single-handedly paid for the renovation of the arts center. But the money is only pledged."

"You think my mother will take it away?"

"I hope not."

Irritation bubbled up in Griffin, both at the insinuation that his mother would be so catty and the knowledge that Jana Stone might revel in a bit of behind-the-scenes vengeance. "I'll talk to her."

"You don't need to get involved."

They reached The Kitchen, leaning closer as Maggie entered the bustling restaurant. "Too late for that, sweetheart."

His aim had been to distract her. Her anxiety was

a palpable force, and he didn't want her to face the crowd in the restaurant showing any kind of weakness.

As soon as he followed her through the door, Griffin realized his mistake. Who was he kidding? As waitstaff and customers at the scuffed Formica tables turned to gawk, he wanted to whisk Maggie away from there to someplace quiet and safe.

He wasn't pretending to be involved to distract her. He cared. A few moments of vulnerability peppered with some spunky attitude and this woman had him wrapped around her little finger.

He was passing through Stonecreek, here to make right his past mistakes. He couldn't afford to care. Not about Maggie Spencer or how she fared in the town. Not about his duplicitous brother or running interference on any possible retribution his mom might try to concoct.

Griffin had made a life for himself away from the quirks of small-town life. First in the army and then as a contractor for various companies around the Pacific Northwest. But the one constant in his life was that he didn't set down roots. Ever.

Maggie was as established in Stonecreek as those hundred-year-old oak trees that bordered the town square. The two of them were oil and water, and it was only going to hurt them both if he didn't cut things off right now.

Then she turned to him, pushing her hair behind her ears and giving him a wisp of a smile filled with gratitude and hope and just the tiniest amount of steel.

Hell, she slayed him.

"We don't have your usual table available," the waitress behind the counter announced, her voice so cold it could freeze water.

"That's okay, Ginnie," Maggie said brightly. "Griffin and I will sit at the counter."

The woman, unfamiliar to Griffin, gave him a long stare. "Are you Griffin Stone?"

"Yep," he said. "I don't believe we've had the pleasure of meeting before. You must be new to Stonecreek."

"Been here five years," the woman said with a sniff. She had blond hair that had been colored blue at the ends, wore heavy black eyeliner and bright red lipstick. Her uniform was a The Kitchen T-shirt and a pair of multicolored leggings under a black miniskirt. She glanced at Maggie, then back to Griffin. "I'm a friend of your brother's. I hope he's doing okay after what happened. Tell him Ginnie sends her love."

Griffin felt Maggie stiffen next to him. He placed a hand on her back, gently guiding her to two empty seats at the counter. "He's fine."

"Wish I could say the same," an older man said from the table behind him.

Griffin glanced over, then did a double take. "Hey, Grady. How's business?"

Grady Wilson had owned the gas station in Stonecreek for as long as Griffin could remember. He used to love to go with his dad for a fill-up because Grady always gave him a piece of licorice from behind the counter. "They opened one of those fancy convenience stores just outside of town. It has a dozen gas pumps and a hundred ways to flavor a soda. I've tried to modernize things, but it's been a struggle." He inclined his head toward Maggie, who sat straight in her chair, pretending to study her menu. "Would have helped me if the town council had refused their application for a lease."

Maggie's lips pursed. "That land was in the next county so not under our domain," she said quietly. "He knows that."

"But that's not as bad as my Gloria's heartbreak after this weekend."

"Mrs. Wilson still teaching?" Griffin asked, not liking where the conversation was headed. Gloria Wilson had been his third-grade teacher and one of the few in his not-so-illustrious academic career to think he had any potential.

Grady shook his head. "Retired last year. Her arthritis got too bad to stand for long periods. Doesn't get out much, but she'd been looking forward to the wedding for months. Your mother was kind enough to invite us."

"*I* invited them," Maggie muttered under her breath.

"She about cried her eyes out Saturday afternoon. I haven't seen her that upset since Ross and Rachel broke up."

"Ross and Rachel got back together," Ginnie added, sliding two waters onto the counter in front of Maggie and Griffin. "I suppose there's always hope."

Griffin watched Maggie draw in a shaky breath, then square her shoulders. She looked directly at Ginnie. "I'll have a grilled-chicken sandwich and a diet soda, please," she said with a forced smile. "And there's no hope for Trevor and me."

"A cheeseburger and fries for me," Griffin said. "Along with a sweet tea."

Maggie turned in her seat. "Please tell Mrs. Wilson

I'm sorry she was upset. I didn't mean to disappoint anyone, but Trevor and I—"

"I heard Trevor was as surprised as the rest of us," a heavyset man called from the pass-through between the diner and the kitchen.

"The two of us made the decision together," Maggie insisted, but there was no fight in her voice.

"Gloria worried this would happen," Grady said, shaking his head. "When those two first got together, she told me it would divide the town when things went south."

Griffin massaged a hand along the back of his neck. "It hasn't divided the town."

"Because everyone around here's on Team Trevor," Ginnie said, leaning over the counter toward him. She smiled as she handed him a glass of tea, then flicked a glance toward Maggie. "No offense."

Maggie nodded, not daring to mention her diet soda. She turned back around in her seat. "None taken, I guess."

"I take offense." Griffin spun on his stool to address the entire restaurant. "And I'm speaking for my entire family. No one is angry with Maggie."

Grady laughed and leaned back in his chair, nudging the man who sat at the table next to him. "Less than a week back in town, and the black sheep is now the family spokesman."

"This was a terrible idea," Maggie said under her breath.

"No." Griffin pointed a finger toward Grady. "I'm not the spokesman, but I've talked to my brother. He doesn't blame Maggie." He pressed his lips together so the words *because the breakup was his fault* wouldn't fall from them. "Would I be here with her if there was bad blood between our families?"

"Why *are* you here with her?" Ginnie asked, folding her arms over her chest.

"We ran into each other on the street," Maggie said quickly, "and were both headed to lunch. It was a co-incidence."

"We're friends," Griffin said simply. Despite how hard she was trying to keep it together, it was obvious Maggie needed a friend right now.

"Your brother is okay with that?" Ginnie raised a heavily penciled brow.

"There's no bad blood," Griffin repeated. He shifted, held out his hands to encompass all of the restaurant patrons. "Everyone hear the news? Spread it around. The Stones and the Spencers are still friends."

"Other than Jason," a voice called from one of the far tables.

"Jason doesn't count," Griffin shot back. "You know that."

Hushed laughter rippled through the room and the tension eased. He turned back around and picked up a french fry from the plate Ginnie had just set before him, popping it into his mouth.

He chewed for a few seconds before turning to Maggie. "This town is too small for its own good."

She gave a tiny nod, her eyes guarded as she stared at him. "Thank you. This time you really did play the hero."

"Don't get used to it," he said and dipped a fry into the ranch dressing drowning the sad pieces of lettuce the cook had seen fit to bestow upon her. "It was a one-time deal. I'm not the tights-wearing type."

Her mouth quirked at the edges. "I'll remember that, although back in high school you had the butt to pull off tights."

"I was a jerk back in high school."

"No argument from me," she said, taking a bite of her sandwich.

"I'm sorry I was a jerk," he said softly and was rewarded with a blush that colored her cheeks the most adorable soft pink hue.

"I'm not sure I forgive you," she said with a small smile, "but I shockingly like the man you've become."

Griffin's heart flipped, and he rubbed a hand against his chest, wholly unused to any activity from that part of his anatomy. It was simple praise, and maybe a little backhanded, but he felt proud to have earned it.

"It's not shocking," he said casually. "I'm irresistible. Everyone knows it. Ask Ginnie. She'll tell you."

Maggie's grin widened as she looked over to the young waitress, who was busy staring at Griffin and not so busy paying attention to her customers.

"I think she's available," Maggie said with a laugh.

"I'm not interested in her," Griffin answered, letting his gaze lower to Maggie's full mouth, then sighing as it pressed into a thin line.

"I should go," she said, her fork dropping to the plate with a clatter. "Now that I've outed myself in town, there are some businesses I need to check in with before the garden center open house this weekend." She pulled out her wallet and grabbed a wad of bills.

"Lunch is my treat," Griffin said, adjusting his ball cap and regretting his inherent need to flirt with this woman. He'd spooked her, which made her ten times smarter than him. The strange connection between them could go nowhere. They both knew it. But Griffin had a lot of experience ignoring things that he should do in favor of things he wanted to do. Apparently, Maggie Spencer was no exception.

"I insist on paying." She slapped some money onto the counter and took a step away. "It's the least I can do since I forced you to have lunch with me."

He laughed. "No one forces me to do anything I don't want to."

Her teeth tugged at her bottom lip. "Okay, then. Be sure to tell your mom that everything is copacetic with our families. I'll work on Grammy."

"Right." Griffin muttered a curse under his breath. He didn't want their families to be involved. He didn't want to admit most of the restaurant was staring at the two of them, and tongues would be wagging throughout town that Maggie had been spotted with the other Stone brother. The black sheep, as Grady had so helpfully pointed out. Griffin didn't want any of this.

Except Maggie. Despite everything else, he wanted Maggie more with each moment they spent together.

"I'll see you around. Thanks, Ginnie," she called, then turned to Grady. "Tell Gloria I'll save her seats in the first row for the benefit concert the high school a cappella group is doing at the garden center this weekend. I know she loves hearing the kids sing." She stepped forward, placed a hand on the man's meaty hand. "I'm really sorry I disappointed her. Sorry about everything."

Grady nodded. "You're still a good girl, Maggie, even if you messed up real bad."

As Griffin watched her walk out of the restaurant, he tamped down the urge to pound his fist into something. Trevor would be fitting. He hated that Maggie was the town good girl, a label she wore like a hair shirt. He hated seeing her apologize for something that wasn't her fault.

Most of all he hated how much he cared. That was a fast track to disaster for everyone.

Maggie plucked the game controller out of her brother's hand a few nights later.

"Give it back," Ben shouted, jumping up from the chair. "I'm going to…" He groaned as a bleating stream of beeps and buzzes came from the television screen. "I died."

"Great," Maggie said with an eye roll. "Now you have time to take out the trash."

Her brother groaned again. "Who died and made you boss?" he asked. He tapped an angry foot on the carpet as an awkward silence filled the air between them. She wasn't the boss, but their mother's death eleven years ago had thrust her into the role of caregiver, for both of her younger siblings. Their father was never much for rules or routines, so Maggie had become the one to keep order in the household.

"You can't spend the entire summer break playing video games."

"Dad doesn't care," Ben shot back.

"He does," Maggie argued. "But he's got the commissioned piece to finish in the next few weeks. He's distracted."

"He's always distracted." Ben grabbed the remote control from the coffee table and turned off the TV. "You just don't see it because you're too busy living your own life."

"I'm here now." Maggie had moved back into her father's house two days ago when she couldn't convince the couple who'd rented her house to find another place. Her stuff had already been in boxes, ready to be moved into Trevor's house on the edge of downtown.

She'd insisted they not move in together until after the wedding, and although Trevor had argued, now she was glad she'd followed her instinct. Her new tenants had rented her house furnished, so she'd only needed to move her personal belongings. It was strange and vaguely depressing to be an adult living in her girlhood room again. Of course, her father hadn't done anything to update the decor, so she had a canopy bed with pink ruffles on the edge of the comforter, random posters of boy band heartthrobs on the walls and her collection of snow globes standing sentry on her old dresser. She needed to change things but couldn't quite find the motivation.

"Nothing will change," Ben grumbled. "You'll get sick of us, and Dad will ignore everything outside his studio. Morgan will be a senior next year so then she'll go to college and I'll be alone."

"You're not alone." Maggie reached forward and brushed Ben's overlong bangs out of his eyes. "I'll take you for a haircut tomorrow."

"What does it matter?" Ben took the controller from her hand and tossed it on the recliner. "My hair, whether I brush my teeth, how many hours of video games I play. It doesn't really matter."

"You brush your teeth, right?" Maggie couldn't help but ask, earning another put-upon groan.

"I'll deal with the trash."

"Take Sadie for a walk, too." Hearing her name,

the springer spaniel lifted her head from her dog bed, yawned, then scratched an ear with her hind leg.

"Fine." He said the word with as much enthusiasm as if she'd asked him to scoop the dog's poop with his bare hands. He whistled, and Sadie hopped up and followed him toward the door.

"Hey, Ben."

He glanced over his shoulder.

"You matter," she said, gratified when he flashed a smile instead of rolling his eyes.

Maggie started toward the kitchen, then gave a yelp of surprise as Morgan stepped out of the laundry at the back of the house.

"He brushes his teeth," her sister reported, picking chipped polish off a fingernail. "But only because he has a crush on some girl in his Spanish class."

"Have you been standing there the whole time?"

"Long enough." Morgan shrugged. "I was separating whites and darks, but hearing you chew out Ben was more interesting."

"I wasn't chewing him out," Maggie sighed. Had she been chewing him out?

"We're doing fine. Ben and I aren't babies anymore. You check in plenty, and when it's important Dad pulls his head out of his—"

"Morgan."

"Dad pulls it together when we need him," her sister amended with a hint of a smile.

Tears pricked at the backs of Maggie's eyes. Was that enough? She'd been so preoccupied with town business and planning the wedding that she'd let her presence in her father's home slip over the past few months. Or years. Had it been years?

She glanced around the kitchen and suppressed another sigh. From the scuffed hardwood floors to the butcher-block counters to the stove with one burner that didn't light, nothing had changed since she went away to college almost a decade earlier. It was the same throughout the rest of the house, decor suspended in time. Her father didn't notice or care, but Maggie thought it was past time he should.

It was obvious he'd been spending more and more time in the studio he'd built behind the house six months before her mother's death. It had taken some lean years, but Jim Spencer was now recognized as one of the foremost bronze sculptors in this part of the country. The piece he was working on now for a private client in San Francisco would pay the mortgage on this place for over a year. His work was his passion, and although he loved his children, he'd never been a particularly attentive father.

"Can't get his head out of the clouds" was how her grammy described it, and Maggie wondered if the absentmindedness was an unconscious defense mechanism. Jim had never paid much attention to the family legacy, a fact that continually niggled at Vivian.

She hadn't stopped encouraging her son to do something "real" with his life until it became clear that Maggie could fill the void and uphold their standing in Stonecreek.

"Grab a box of pasta while I heat the water," Maggie told her sister. "I like your hair."

Morgan touched her hand to the blue strands like she was surprised to find them on her head. "Grammy wanted me go back to my boring natural color for the wedding."

"I didn't know that," Maggie said apologetically. "I think she means well."

"Because you're her favorite," Morgan said as she emerged from the pantry. "The rest of us are constant disappointments. Especially me."

Jim Spencer walked into the kitchen, wiping his hands on a towel. "You're not a disappointment to anyone. I'll talk to your grandmother." He dropped a kiss on the top of Morgan's blue-hued head. "You're perfect, Mo-mo."

Maggie breathed a sigh of relief. Her father might be scatterbrained and bordering on negligent, but he had his moments.

"I'm sick of people calling me that stupid nickname."

"I can call you whatever I like. How about Princess Morgana of the Butterfly Fairy Convention?"

Maggie smiled. Of the three Spencer kids, Morgan was the most like their father in terms of imagination. She'd spent hours as a child playing dress up and insisting on being referred to by her chosen identity of the week.

"Even worse," Morgan said with a groan. She handed Maggie the box of pasta.

"Are you making dinner tonight?" Jim asked Maggie. "You don't have to do that. I had a plan."

"Quesadillas?" Maggie asked, and Morgan hid her smile.

"What's wrong with cheese and tortillas?" Jim put his hands on his hips.

"Just changing things up a bit," Maggie answered. "I appreciate you letting me stay here, Dad."

"It's your home."

Emotion welled in Maggie's chest. "Grammy came to visit me at the office earlier."

"She mentioned that when she stopped by here," Jim said, looking sheepish when Maggie gasped.

"She talked to you about me?"

"Your grandmother loves you," he said by way of explanation.

Morgan snorted.

"She loves all of you," Jim amended, pulling a bottle of wine off the wrought iron baker's rack in the corner.

"She has to love me," Ben said, entering the room with Sadie trotting along at his ankles. "I'm the only one who can carry on the Spencer name."

"Don't be a Neanderthal." Morgan popped the top on a can of soda and took a long drink.

"Shouldn't you be having milk?" Maggie asked automatically.

Morgan held up the can in mock salute. "I liked you better when you were worried about Ben's teeth."

Their father paused in the act of pouring a glass of wine. "What's wrong with Ben's teeth?"

"Why am I a Neanderthal?" Ben swiped the soda can from Morgan, gulped it down, then burped loudly.

"He needs to brush regularly," Maggie told her father.

"I could have a baby on my own," Morgan said, swatting Ben on the back of the head. "My kid would have the Spencer name that way."

Jim jabbed a finger at Morgan. "No babies," he said, then sipped his wine. "Brush your teeth," he told his son.

"I told you he shows up when we need him," Morgan said to Maggie.

Jim narrowed his eyes. "Did you doubt it?"

Maggie's gaze hitched on the wine label. "Is that my wedding wine?"

"Don't want it to go to waste," her father said. "May I pour you a glass?"

"I had lunch at The Kitchen," Maggie said instead of answering. The thought of even a sip of the wine that had been bottled to celebrate her wedding made her stomach ache. But her father meant well so she didn't want to refuse outright.

"You definitely need a drink," he said and pulled out a second glass.

"Ben stole my soda and it was the last one," Morgan complained. "I should probably have wine, too."

"Only in church on Sundays," Jim countered.

Morgan scrunched up her nose. "We don't go to church."

"Then no wine. Listen to your sister and have some milk."

Maggie felt her shoulders begin to tremble and tears prick her eyes. She pressed three fingers to her mouth to prevent a full-blown sob from escaping, then dragged in a shaky breath and swiped at her cheeks.

Silence filled the room as the three members of her immediate family turned to stare at her.

"I love you guys," she whispered, squeezing shut her eyes. She needed to hold it together, but the stress of the past few days was too much. She might not be heartbroken, but she was humiliated, and the normalcy of her family's silly banter reminded her she wasn't going through this alone.

"It's going to be okay," her father said, wrapping his big body around her. He smelled like the clay he used to make the original sculptures that would then be cast into bronze. The earthy, musty scent would always remind her of home.

Morgan and Ben hugged her, too. "We love you, too," her sister said, adding the scent of patchouli to the mix.

"I could shank Trevor," Ben offered, "for whatever he did to make you into a runaway bride." Maggie smiled through her tears as she felt her brother wipe his nose on the sleeve of her shirt. Teenage boys were truly disgusting.

"No babies, wine or shanking," Jim said. "I might not run the tightest ship, but even I have lines you can't cross."

"The water's boiling over," Maggie said as she heard a sizzle from the stove. She pulled away from the family hug. "Dinner will be ready in about ten minutes."

"I'll make a salad," Morgan offered.

"I'll set the table," Ben added, playfully bumping Morgan out of the way as he moved toward the cabinets that held the plates and bowls.

Another wave of love swelling through her, Maggie dumped the pasta into the water and adjusted the burner's heat. Her father handed her a glass of wine when she turned to him.

"Don't say he didn't deserve me." She shook her head as she touched the glass to her lips. The pinot noir was fruity and light, with just the right amount of depth at the end. "I've heard that line too many times already."

"You deserve someone who can make you truly happy," Jim said instead, clinking his glass to hers.

"To your happiness, Maggie May, no matter how long it takes you to find it."

Maggie smiled and tried not to burst into tears again. "Thanks, Dad."

Chapter Seven

Brenna crossed her arms over her chest. "Are you trying to get in my pants?"

Marcus Sanchez paused in the act of pulling wrapped sandwiches from the brown paper bag he'd set on the tasting room counter.

"It's a turkey sandwich," he said, studying the bundle in his hands. "I'll admit the aioli is a nice touch, but it's not exactly seduction-worthy."

She kept her gaze focused on the sandwich and not Marcus's dark eyes and kind face. "You're being nice to me."

When he didn't respond, she eventually glanced up. One side of his mouth curved. "I like you."

Three words but they packed the wallop of a punch to her emotions, washing through her and wearing down most of her razor-sharp defenses. For the past four days Marcus had singled her out with some small act of kindness. First, it had been a vase of flowers on her desk, then yesterday he'd arrived at the office with a cup of her standing drink order from Espresso's Coffee Shop in town and now he'd brought lunch from her favorite deli.

Brenna was starving. Fridays in the summer were always busy at the vineyard, and she had almost a dozen reservations for the tasting room. She tried her best to make the space welcoming with twinkling lights and fresh flowers but it was difficult to ignore that her desk was just on the other side of the temporary partition that separated the room. She'd be scrambling until the planned renovations were complete.

Marcus handed her a sandwich, and she blushed as her stomach growled. "This doesn't have to be complicated," he told her. "I know you don't stop for lunch when things are swamped around here." He gestured to the empty seats at the counter in front of her. "You have a break so let's eat."

But it *was* complicated because Brenna had learned over and over that nothing good in life came without a price. From her mother's stingy, selfish love to the way Ellie's father had walked out as soon as Brenna told him she was pregnant. She'd thought Trevor was telling her the truth about his devotion to Maggie, and that had turned out disastrously.

Her interactions with him this week had been coolly awkward. He'd actually called her into his office on Monday afternoon to tell her he didn't blame her for telling Maggie the whole truth and assured her the scene at the church wouldn't affect her position at Harvest.

But she still blamed herself for being a fool and a terrible friend to Maggie. She wanted nothing to do with Trevor Stone, but Marcus was another story entirely. It was strange after a year of having him ignore her that suddenly he wanted to be her friend.

"I don't trust this," she murmured.

"The sandwich or the chips that go with it?"

She shook her head. "You have no reason to be nice to me."

He laughed softly. "I didn't realize I needed one."

"You know what I mean." She turned and busied herself with rearranging wineglasses on the shelf behind her.

"Brenna."

"I don't deserve anyone being nice to me right now."

He stepped around the counter, placed a gentle hand over hers to still her movements. "I can tell that last weekend is tearing you up inside."

She gave a jerky nod. "I should have told her."

"You made a mistake."

"A bad one."

"We all make mistakes."

She turned to him, bile rising in her throat at the thought of all the stupid choices she'd made over the years. "You're a good person, Marcus. Everyone knows it."

His hand was warm and comforting on hers, and she closed her eyes when he squeezed her fingers. "I was married once," he said quietly.

He still gripped her hand but when she glanced toward him he was staring at the shelf of wineglasses like he couldn't stand to meet her gaze.

"For how long?"

"Five years. I was working at a vineyard in Sonoma at the time. She worked in town as a waitress. She'd come from a big family and wanted lots of kids."

"You didn't?"

He shrugged. "The vines were my babies, so I didn't think much about it. But I wanted her to be happy."

"Of course you did." Brenna tugged at her hand, but Marcus held tight.

"It took eighteen months of trying for her to get pregnant, and she miscarried at nine weeks."

"I'm sorry," Brenna whispered.

He turned to her then, and his eyes were filled with a mix of regret and sorrow. "It broke her, and I couldn't deal with it. I left the hospital, drove to a bar, got drunk on the cheapest liquor I could find, then went home with a woman I met that night." His features were granite as if he couldn't afford to let any vulnerability show. But his eyes gave away everything, and Brenna's heart broke for him.

"A big mistake."

He swallowed, his throat bobbing. "She left me, and once I pulled myself together I moved to Oregon. Took a job at Harvest a few months later. She remarried and the last I heard they have three little ones." His lips pressed into a thin line. "And I still have the vines."

"Oh, Marcus." Brenna turned her hand over in his and linked their fingers.

"Don't think for a minute you have the market cornered on regret." He reached out and lifted a strand of her hair, watching it trail across his skin like it was the most fascinating thing he'd ever seen. "Let me be nice to you, Brenna. Not because I have an ulterior motive. Not because I'm in any position to pass judgment."

He took a step back when a car door slammed outside the office door, untangling their fingers and shoving his hands into his pockets. "I like you, and I like having some-one to be nice to again."

She bit down on her lip, so much she wanted to say to him but the words wouldn't form.

The chimes above the front door opened and two couples walked in, laughing and talking among them-selves. Her next reservation.

"Take the sandwich, okay?" Marcus gave her a pleading look.

She nodded, then turned to the foursome. "Welcome to Harvest Vineyards. Have a seat, everyone."

Marcus backed away, but she stepped closer to him, ignoring the customers for a moment. "Would you like to have dinner tonight?"

His brows rose and he glanced behind him like there might be someone else she was inviting.

"Yes, I'm talking to you." She flashed a smile. "It will be me and Ellie so nothing fancy. You're welcome to join us if you don't have plans."

"Is this a pity invite?" he asked, those dark eyes narrowing. "Because I told you about my awful mistake?"

She let her smile gentle. "It's an invite because I like you."

He seemed to relax at that. "What time?"

"Six," she said sheepishly. "Ellie still goes to bed early."

"Text me your address, and I'll be there."

"Okay." She clutched her hands in front of her stom-ach and watched him disappear around the partition. Then she stashed the sandwich and brown bag behind the counter.

"Let's start the weekend with our signature pinot

noir," she announced to the two couples. "It's going to be a great Friday here at Harvest."

Trevor stalked into his mother's kitchen the following Saturday morning.

"Where's Mom?" Trevor threw out the question, then veered toward the refrigerator in the family home that housed every generation of Stones since Stonecreek's founding.

Griffin returned his attention to the set of plans spread out in front of him on the dining room table. "She went to town to check in with the staff running the Pioneer Day booth."

"Did you drink the last of the coffee?" Trevor held up the stainless steel pot like he wanted to brain Griffin with it. "Mom always saves me a cup on Saturdays."

Griffin lifted a shoulder. "You should have gotten here earlier. I supplied coffee to the guys who showed up to help with pruning this morning."

"I'm off the clock on the weekend." Trevor set the coffeepot in the sink with a clatter.

"It's a vineyard. We're never off the clock."

"That's rich," Trevor shot back, "coming from the man who was gone for the better part of a decade." He moved closer and stared at the teenage boy standing just behind Griffin. "Who are you?"

"Cole Maren," the boy answered.

"What are you doing here?"

Cole adjusted the bill of his ball cap. "I work here."

"In my mother's house?"

Griffin pushed back from the table and stood. "What's with the interrogation, Trev? You can see the kid is here with me. He's going to run into town and pick up some supplies I need for excavation. The machinery arrives on Monday."

"Why do you want his help?" Trevor demanded.

"Is there a problem?"

"You know who his dad is, right?"

"Dude," Cole muttered, moving to put on his sweatshirt. "I don't need this."

"Don't go anywhere." Griffin placed a hand on Cole's shoulder. "I need your help.

"The office," he said to Trevor, nudging his brother out of the way as he moved past.

As soon as Trevor shut the door to the home office that had been their father's sanctuary, Griffin rounded on him. "What the hell was that about?"

"Toby Maren is the town drunk," Trevor said like that explained everything.

Griffin snorted. "You mean in all these years we still only have one?"

"The family is bad news. I heard Cole's brother is doing time over in Elbert County for assault and robbery. I don't think the mom is in the picture. So he's grown up with an alcoholic and a criminal." Trevor threw up his hands. "Where does that leave him?"

"In need of a decent role model?"

"You sound like Marcus," Trevor said with a derisive sniff. "Neither one of you has a sense of what's right. We have an image to protect at Harvest—our brand means quality. That means we need to employ quality people."

"You don't know Cole enough to say that he's not."

"I know he's trouble. Why can't you trust me on this? You don't have a clue what goes on in this town anymore. You can't just waltz back in here after a decade and act like you're going to take over."

Color flooded Trevor's face as he paced from one end of the wood-paneled office to the other. He and his brother had never been close, but Trevor had a point when he said that he'd stayed while Griffin had left the family business behind. Griffin wanted to show some respect for the years Trevor had put into building Harvest's market share. A great wine wasn't worth its grapes if no one discovered it.

"I'm not a threat to you," he said. "Mom wants me to build the tasting room, and I'm going to do that for her. Then I'll be gone."

"You had lunch with Maggie last week," Trevor said, his tone accusing.

Griffin's spine stiffened. "So what?"

"Why?" Trevor asked with a glare.

"I ran into her in town. We were both hungry."

"Give me a break." A muscle ticked in Trevor's jaw. "First you play her knight in shining armor after the wedding and now you're going on lunch dates? Are you suddenly interested in my girl?"

Anger bubbled up in Griffin along with an overwhelming sense of possession. "She isn't yours," he said through clenched teeth.

"Well, she sure as hell isn't going to go for someone like you." Trevor's eyes narrowed. "Maggie cares about her image and her family's reputation too much to start a scandal."

"That fact worked to your benefit after you cheated on her," Griffin said quietly.

"It's over," Trevor insisted. "Turns out there's nothing between Julia and me." He rubbed a hand over his jaw. "It was a mistake but also a blessing. Maggie wouldn't have made me happy."

"What would, Trev? You're mad that I'm working at the vineyard. You can't stand that I'm giving a kid a chance." Griffin lifted his hand, ticking off the list of grievances his brother seemed to have against him. "You don't like that I had lunch with Maggie. From the outside, you've got it pretty good. A great job, a breakup where you came out smelling like roses, even though the whole thing was your fault. Life is handing you pitchers of lemonade and you're pining for lemons. What exactly would make you happy?"

Trevor opened his mouth, then snapped it shut again. "Keep an eye on Cole Maren. I have a bad feeling about him." He stalked past Griffin and out of the room.

Griffin returned to the kitchen, his temper practically boiling over, then blew out a breath when Cole shoved a piece of paper in front of his face.

"I took your notes and made a list of the lumber and supplies we'll need to get started on the project. My dad used to work for the garbage company, so I called and arranged for them to drop off a Dumpster on Monday." He gave a small smile that looked more like a grimace. "If you don't think we need it, I can use one of the vineyard's trucks to haul away the waste."

"A Dumpster will make things faster." Griffin scanned the list. "You've done a good job here."

"Mr. Stone is wrong about me," Cole said, his words steely. "But he's right about my dad and brother."

Griffin raised a brow.

"Yeah, I eavesdropped," the boy admitted. "Only because I wanted to hear what he'd say so I'd know how to convince you to let me keep this job."

"You don't need to convince me." Griffin folded the piece of paper in half and handed it back to him. "I was a teenager once, and you can't help your family."

"I couldn't believe when Mr. Sanchez hired me for the summer. I'd applied for jobs all over town." He shook his head. "Then you picked me to help you with the construction."

"You practically threw yourself at me," Griffin said with a chuckle. He was planning on handling most of the work himself but needed a few laborers to do the heavy lifting. When he'd asked the field manager if he had any workers to spare, Cole had tripped all over himself to volunteer.

"I like building things," Cole said simply but there was an underlying meaning to the words. This was a kid who'd seen plenty of things in his life torn apart. He was tall, almost six feet with gangly arms, long legs and hair that was badly in need of a cut. He favored black metal band T-shirts and ripped jeans. Overall, he looked like another punk kid with a surly attitude. Much like Griffin had when he was that age. Maybe that was why he saw something more in Cole. Potential. Hope. Determination. Characteristics he recognized and respected even if Trevor couldn't.

"Take the truck and pick up this stuff from Kurt's. The vineyard has an account."

Cole nodded. "Then what?"

"It's Saturday." Griffin smiled. "Don't you have some lucky girl to take out for the night?"

The teen rolled his bright blue eyes. "The girls who run in my crowd are skanks."

"Hey." Griffin reached out and cuffed the back of

the boy's head. "Treat women with respect. Talk about them with respect."

"But they don't—"

"You should know better than most that what you do matters more than what the people around you do. Be the man you want others to see you as. Maybe you'll find a girl who wants to be with the best version of who you are."

Cole rolled his eyes. "Dr. Phil much?"

"That was some of my best stuff," Griffin countered with a laugh. "I have wisdom to impart, young apprentice."

"How's that advice working for *you*?"

Irritation scratched just under Griffin's skin, mainly because the question made too many of his own doubts crawl out of their dark caves yearning for the light. Returning to Stonecreek had turned his life upside down. He was back in his family home, trying hard not to become invested in the vineyard even as his fingers itched to work the vines.

He lusted after Maggie Spencer, a woman all wrong for him and not just because a week ago she'd been in a wedding gown ready to marry his brother. "This isn't about me," he mumbled.

"I know Morgan Spencer." Cole stared at a spot over Griffin's shoulder. "She's not like her sister—doesn't care about the Spencer name and all that."

Griffin rubbed the back of his neck, grateful for any change in topic, no matter how minuscule. "Are you friends?"

"Sort of. Maybe. Not really. She thinks she's some kind of rebel, but she's better than she pretends to be. Better than most of the guys in this town deserve."

"She has that in common with her sister," Griffin said, thinking of himself and Maggie.

"Yeah?" Cole asked and his young eyes held an understanding far beyond his years.

Griffin sighed. "Yeah."

Chapter Eight

Maggie felt like her cheeks might break if she held her tight smile for one more second.

She excused herself from the group she'd joined a few minutes earlier, and moved toward the one quiet corner of the town square. She lowered herself onto a park bench and leaned back, watching as folks streamed toward the strands of lights that marked the festival's midway.

The Pioneer Day Festival was in full force, and Maggie had been making the rounds for the past three hours. Before that she'd spent most of the morning helping to set up booths and unload food and supplies from the backs of trucks. Normally, she loved the start of festival season in Stonecreek. The town could find a reason to celebrate almost anything, and the summer calendar was crowded with weekends of barbecue, pies, flowers and art.

Even before Maggie had become mayor she'd volunteered for setup and teardown at almost every event. But today the camaraderie felt forced, her conversations with old friends stilted. Jason Stone had been holding court at the morning's pancake breakfast, which kicked off the festival, like he was already the front-runner in the election.

Maggie had found herself on the periphery of her beloved community. Ever since she'd ventured out to lunch with Griffin, people had been friendly but still standoffish, as if she had some sort of "tarnished bride" germs that might rub off on them if they got too close. Apparently, she'd taken for granted her position as "Stonecreek's sweetheart" and how one mistake could push her off that platform like a disgraced pirate shuffling along the plank.

"Shouldn't you be shaking hands or kissing babies?"

She turned as Griffin approached from the far side of the park, hands jammed into the pockets of his jeans. As always, he looked effortlessly handsome in a gray chambray shirt and dark jeans.

"I've already left lipstick marks on all the talcum powder–scented heads. My work here tonight is done."

"Then my timing is excellent."

Shivers of awareness spiking through her, she patted the bench. "Have a seat," she said, hoping she sounded casual as opposed to as nervous as a schoolgirl.

Griffin had always had that effect on her, even when they were younger and he'd made it his mission in life to ignore her. It didn't matter where she'd been as a teenager or how many people were surrounding her; as soon as Griffin had appeared her body had hummed liked a high-voltage power line.

"Do things ever change around here?" he asked as he dropped down next to her. "Pioneer Day looks the same as it did when we were kids."

Maggie smiled. That was one of the things she loved about festival season—the tradition of it. "Two years ago," she said solemnly, "the cooks at The Kitchen used a new batter recipe for their funnel cakes. They came out of the fryers as gelatinous grease blobs. Caused quite a stir and was the lead story in the community newspaper the next week."

"Lesson learned, I hope."

"Oh, yes." Maggie nodded and worked to keep her expression serious. "Back to the original batter the following year and they offered half-price funnel cakes on opening night to make it up to everyone."

Griffin laughed softly. "No wonder people around here are obsessed with your nonwedding. Nothing else has happened in years."

"Maybe I could orchestrate a minor zombie outbreak. That would take the attention off me."

"It's worth a shot."

She breathed in the cool air of evening, tinged with the scents of fried food and cotton candy. Griffin had the gift of helping her not take herself or the town too seriously. Through his perspective she was able to see how trivial some of her worries were in the bigger picture.

She turned her head to look at him. "What brings you into town if you weren't planning on attending the festival?"

"You," he said, keeping his gaze forward. "I didn't have a plan, but I wanted to see you."

Joy rushed through her like an electric current, making her body heat from the inside out. "I'm glad."

He cleared his throat. "Do you want to walk through the festival?"

"Not one bit," she admitted, earning a wide grin.

"What a relief," he said, standing and taking her hand. "Let's go."

She felt only a moment's hesitation that she might be shirking her duty to the town as its mayor.

Wasn't she obligated to attend every minute of every event sponsored in Stonecreek? That was how she'd lived her life for the past two years and, honestly, it was difficult to remember a time before responsibility was her norm.

Glancing at her hand joined with Griffin's, Maggie realized she wanted something different than the norm. She wanted excitement, adventure. More than anything, she wanted Griffin Stone.

"Hurry," she whispered, giggling for the first time in forever. "I need to get out of here before someone sees me."

They ran down the sidewalk, hand in hand, and Maggie felt freer with every step. She knew they weren't doing anything crazy or rebellious, but in her structured world, it felt like a revolution and she reveled in the moment.

By the time they got to the Land Cruiser, parked several blocks away, adrenaline coursed through her veins. Griffin released her hand to open the passenger door and she climbed in, placing a hand over her chest like she could calm her racing heart.

"You're beautiful," Griffin told her, tucking a strand of hair behind her ear. He gave her the cocky half grin that had practically melted her panties in high school, and tonight it made her feel like she might spontaneously combust.

"Oh" was the only response she could manage.

"Oh, yeah," he murmured, his grin widening. He came around the front of the SUV and got behind the wheel, and then they were turning the corner that led to the highway out of town.

"So what's the plan?" she asked, proud her voice didn't tremble.

"Do we need a plan?" Griffin drummed his fingers casually on the console between them. His hands were large, his fingers long and surprisingly elegant even with several scratches and scars. She liked seeing the evidence of his labor on his body.

"I never do anything without a plan."

"There's always a first time."

"But you have a plan," she insisted.

He laughed and turned on the radio. "Yes, Maggie May. I have a plan." Glancing over at her, he cocked a brow. "But I'm going to leave you in suspense."

"I hate suspense."

He laughed again, then began to sing along with the song on the radio. It was a classic rock anthem from the late seventies, and Maggie closed her eyes as she listened to Griffin's rich baritone strike the perfect harmony with the lead singer. She joined in when the chorus started, letting the music and the moment sweep her away. At least until she realized that Griffin had gone silent.

"What?" she said when she turned and found him staring at her.

"Finally, something you're not good at," he said with a mischievous smile. "I was beginning to think you were too perfect, but, Maggie Spencer, you couldn't carry a tune out of a bucket."

She gasped and leaned forward to flip off the radio. "It's no wonder you don't have a girlfriend when you're dishing out that kind of charm."

Silence filled the vehicle's interior for only a few seconds before she heard the deep rumble of Griffin's laughter. As much as embarrassment heated her cheeks, Maggie felt a smile pull at the corners of her mouth. "That was so rude," she muttered.

"You're adorable," he said, reaching a hand over and patting her leg. She wore a fitted blouse and crisp knee-length skirt so the feel of his calloused fingers against her bare skin sent awareness racing through her. "I like that you aren't perfect."

"I'm not that terrible of a singer," she insisted. He didn't answer and after a moment she huffed out an irritated breath. "Okay, I'm awful but it's still bad manners for you to point it out."

She stared at the rolling hills and open farmland. They were heading west toward the coast, and the landscape was slowly moving from verdant valley with mountains looming in the distance to the rockier geography of the Oregon coast.

"You're real." He turned the radio on again, humming along with a popular country hit. "That's way more interesting than your Stonecreek image if you ask me. Sing at the top of your lungs. I could care less if it sounds like a herd of cats dying a slow death."

She burst out laughing. "It's a good thing you're so darn hot," she said when she could control her laughter enough to speak. "Otherwise, women would run the other way as soon as you opened your mouth."

"Are you going to run?" he asked, his tone suddenly serious.

"No," she said without hesitation. She hadn't felt this happy in a long time. "But I am going to subject you to my singing." She turned up the volume knob on the radio as a Carrie Underwood song started. "I love this song so much."

Griffin grimaced but she could tell he liked her answer. It was close to seven when he pulled off the highway onto a two-lane road that followed the coastline. She rolled down her window and breathed deeply of the ocean-scented air.

"I don't know this town," she said, gazing at the clapboard houses and faded shingled buildings. There were huge pots of trailing vines and flowers situated on every block, and a few couples and several families meandered along the sidewalks. It was quaint and quiet and exactly the kind of place Maggie was in the mood to discover.

He parked the car in front of a cozy-looking used bookstore. "Lychen is more a town for locals than tourists. It's a fishing village really, but the people here are great."

They got out of the Land Cruiser and Griffin scanned the street. "It's grown some since I came here in high school, but it still looks pretty sleepy."

"How did you discover it?" She held up a hand. "Wait. I bet it was a girl."

He smiled sheepishly. "There were plenty of girls, but not here." He put a hand on her back to direct her onto the sidewalk, then kept it there as they walked. The light contact reverberated through Maggie.

"My dad and I got in an argument one weekend,

which was not uncommon. By the time I was in high school, it seemed like all we did was fight. That time was different because I'd just gotten my license. I finally had the freedom to leave, so I did."

"And you came to Lychen?"

He nodded. "Not on purpose at first. I had that old Chevy—"

"I remember," she murmured.

"I started driving and this is where I ended up. It was different than Stonecreek. At home I was the kid with an attitude. Everyone had me pegged and I did plenty to live down to their low expectations. But here, no one knew me. I could be whoever I wanted to be. I liked it, you know?"

She glanced over at him, taking in his strong jaw and the tiny lines fanning out from the corners of his eyes. Griffin was different than the boy she'd known growing up. He'd changed in the years he was away from Stonecreek, matured in a way she still could barely grasp.

"Who were you in Lychen?"

"Anonymous," he answered immediately. "I wasn't part of the Stone family. Generations of history didn't weigh me down. I was just a kid with a truck from out of town."

She bit down on her lower lip. How could she and Griffin have grown up so similarly but end up with such opposite views of what the past meant? "I always liked the history," she admitted. "Knowing where I came from gave me a sense of who I was supposed to be."

Griffin's shoulder bumped hers and she felt the heat of his body. The air was cooler on the coast, and she wanted to move closer and wrap herself in his warmth. "I guess I needed to figure it out on my own," he said with a shrug.

They stopped outside a storefront, and he pointed to the sign above the door. Luigi's Italian Inn.

"An original name for a restaurant," she offered.

"I used to walk by this place back in the day and salivate over the smells drifting out, but I didn't have the money for a sit-down dinner back then."

"It smells wonderful."

"What do you think? Spaghetti dinner?"

As if on cue, her stomach growled. She nodded and followed him into the restaurant, breathing in the scent of tangy sauce and yeasty bread. The restaurant was long and narrow, with booths lining the length of one wall. A woman with dark hair and kind eyes greeted them at the hostess stand.

"Welcome to Luigi's. I'm Bianca, the owner, and I'm proud to say we've been serving my *nonna*'s Sicilian recipes here for over thirty years."

Maggie stifled a laugh. "We're all about family history."

Griffin held up two fingers. "A table, please?"

"Our most romantic," Bianca answered with a wink. "It's clear this is a special date." She pointed at Maggie. "You have that look about you."

"I don't have a look," Maggie said automatically. She crossed her arms over her chest, embarrassed to be called out by a stranger. "No look. None."

The woman only laughed and gestured for them to follow her.

"I like your look," Griffin whispered as they moved

through the restaurant, his breath tickling the back of her neck.

What was she doing here? They'd only driven an hour but this place seemed like a lifetime away from Stonecreek.

Maybe that was the gift of this night and this tiny town. Like Griffin had experienced as a teen, she could be whomever she wanted without worrying about what anyone else would think.

They were seated at an intimate booth near the back of the restaurant. A red-checked tablecloth covered the table, and a votive candle flickered from its center. Bianca handed them each a menu.

"Would you like to see the wine list?" she asked, prompting Maggie to raise a brow at Griffin.

"We'll take a bottle of your favorite pinot noir," he responded.

The woman nodded approvingly. "Right away."

"What if it's not from Harvest?" Maggie asked when they were alone.

He laughed softly. "I think I'll manage."

She sat back against the booth's cushion. "If Trevor and I ordered wine at a restaurant, he insisted that it be from Harvest. He wouldn't drink anything else."

One side of Griffin's full mouth quirked. "Then he's missing out and besides—"

He broke off as the owner returned, presenting a bottle to Griffin. "I have one of Harvest Vineyards' best vintages. The volcanic soil makes the grapes especially crisp. I don't know if you're familiar with Harvest…"

Griffin nodded. "Vaguely."

"They're a rising star in the Oregon wine industry and also family owned, which we appreciate."

"I think we can trust your judgment." Griffin looked to Maggie for approval. "Sound good to you?"

"Of course."

The woman uncorked the wine and Griffin went through the process of inspecting the cork, then swirled and sniffed his sample before taking a sip. Amusement danced in his green eyes. "Very nice. A bit of cherry and currant. The tannins and acid are well-balanced."

"You know your wine," the owner murmured approvingly, pouring a generous amount for Maggie and then filling Griffin's glass. "We have a special that would pair beautifully with it. It's a poached salmon with goat cheese and asparagus, plus a side of mushroom risotto."

"Maggie?" Griffin asked, and the fact that he so easily deferred to her made her knees go weak. Other parts of her body gathered strength, like lusty soldiers standing at attention.

"Sure." She nodded, pressing her lips together. The woman could have offered her monkey brains and she would have agreed to it. Her head was in a fog; the fact that Griffin had no problem letting her take the lead was as attractive as his handsome face and killer body.

Despite being a grown woman and mayor of Stonecreek, Maggie felt like she spent most of her time deferring to other people's wishes. From her grandmother's expectations to Trevor's strict ideas about how their relationship should progress, Maggie rarely got to choose something solely for herself. Even when she went out to dinner in town, she consciously made the rounds of local restaurants so she'd be seen supporting a variety of businesses.

"Would you like a salad to start?"

"Yes," she said with probably more force than necessary as Bianca took a small step back.

"A house salad would be great," Maggie said, softening her tone. "Balsamic dressing, please."

The owner nodded and looked toward Griffin. "I'll have the same thing," he told her.

When Bianca walked away again, Griffin inclined his head. "You feel passionate about salad."

"I guess," Maggie said, feeling color rise to her cheeks once again. She took a long sip of wine. "It's good. Did you know they carried Harvest here?"

"Not specifically, but most of the coastal towns do. Trevor is good at his job."

"He's driven," she agreed. "But I don't want to talk about anything to do with Stonecreek tonight. Tell me about your time in the army."

"A light topic," he murmured. "Nice."

She rolled her eyes. "I never really understood what made you join in the first place," she admitted. "I remember that you'd been accepted to Oregon State. I thought you were going into business and—"

He held up a hand. "Me, too. But Dad and I had that last fight after the fire. He told me there was no way he'd let me work at Harvest. I was angry and hurt, although I probably deserved it."

"The fire was an accident."

"A cigarette left to burn next to a pile of magazines. My stupid friends and I had gone in to grab a few bottles of wine."

"Not many teenagers get drunk on quality wine."

"Totally unable to appreciate it at that age." Griffin picked up his glass, twirled the stem in his fingers.

"Especially when most nights ended with someone puking in the bushes."

"You learned a hard lesson."

"Dad didn't see it that way." He frowned. "In his opinion, I'd done it to sabotage the vineyard. They were hosting the Northwest Winemakers conference the following week."

"Everyone knew it wasn't on purpose."

"It didn't matter what anyone else thought. I understood at that moment that even if he relented—and Mom was going to do her best to make sure he did—even if he deigned to find a place for me at the vineyard, I couldn't work for him. Our relationship was toxic."

"There's a huge jump between not wanting to work for the family business and skipping college to join the army."

Griffin took a long drink of wine. "Not so big when you're an angry teen wanting to stick it to your parents." He shrugged. "The army was actually the best thing that could have happened to me at that point. It gave me purpose and structure—two things I didn't realize I wanted in my life."

A waitress brought their salads, and Maggie forked up a bite of lettuce, then pointed it at Griffin. "See, structure and planning have their benefits."

He clinked his fork against hers. "Touché, Maggie May."

Her name on his lips felt like a caress, and Maggie wanted to lean into it. Away from Stonecreek, she felt light and free. She could do anything, even explore her attraction to a man who could never be right for her.

They talked more about his time in the army and all

the places he'd visited. Listening to Griffin, Maggie realized how narrow her life had been. She'd gone to school an hour from Stonecreek and, other than a senior trip to London with her grandmother, she'd barely traveled past the Oregon state line.

Griffin didn't seem bothered by her lack of worldliness. He asked questions about her family and her role as mayor, seeming genuinely interested in her ideas about the town's future.

Maggie didn't want the night to end.

Griffin couldn't remember the last time he'd felt so happy. Had Maggie been this amazing when they were younger? Probably... Although he'd been too stupid and self-centered to see it.

He took her hand as they stood overlooking the beach on the town pier, lacing his fingers with hers. He'd never touch her so casually in Stonecreek, where curious eyes were everywhere. But here it was the two of them, and he wanted to make the most of every minute.

"I should come to the coast more often," she said, her chest rising and falling as she breathed in the salty air. "The sound of the ocean is the best."

"Next time we'll walk the beach before we eat." They'd lingered over dinner, and it was dark when they'd exited the restaurant. But the moon was almost full, so they could still see the waves crashing against the sand.

"Next time," she repeated quietly, then turned to him. "What's going on here, Griffin?"

He ran a hand through his hair, keeping his gaze

straight ahead. "I'm on an amazing date with an amazing woman and—"

"This isn't a date," she interrupted, tugging her hand from his.

His gut tightened. Those weren't the words he'd wanted or expected to hear from her.

Now he shifted, looking down into her gray eyes. Strands of lights lined the pier, so he could see that her gaze was guarded…serious. Not at all the easygoing, playful woman who'd sat across from him at dinner.

"What would you call it?"

"I'm not sure," she admitted.

"But you're confident it's not a date?"

She shook her head. "I'm not confident of anything at the moment. You might remember my life turned completely upside down last week. But even if that wasn't a factor, I can't imagine you wanting to go on a date with me."

"I'm not the same guy I used to be."

She laughed softly. "Well, thank heavens for that."

"I'm sorry," he blurted. "For who I was back then."

"I get that you were an angry kid and the whole 'rebel without a cause' bit."

She did air quotes with her fingers, making light of his teenage angst, which he definitely deserved. The things he'd seen after leaving Stonecreek made him understand how good he'd had it growing up.

That perspective allowed him to return, made him want to make amends with his mother. Even had him wishing he could have another chance with his dad.

"What was it about me in particular that you hated?"

The question caught him off guard and he felt his mouth drop open. "I didn't hate you," he muttered.

"Really?" Her delicate brows furrowed, and a line formed between her eyes that he wanted to smooth away with his fingertip. "Because the way I remember it you relished being churlish to everyone but I was in a special category."

He rubbed a hand along the back of his neck. "I hated myself," he admitted softly. "And I was jealous of you. You were perfect. Everyone in town loved you. It was clear even back then that you were the golden girl of Stonecreek, which meant you represented everything I could never hope to be."

"But now I'm okay because my crown has been knocked off?"

"That's not it," he said, needing her to understand. He paced to the edge of the pier, then back to her. "I can't explain it but there's a connection between us, Maggie. I know you feel it."

She glanced out to the ocean in front of them. "I do."

"I think maybe I realized it back then. Except you were younger and friends with Trevor and so far out of my league." He chuckled. "That part hasn't changed. But I'm not the same person, and I want a chance with you."

"It's complicated," she said softly. "A week ago I was supposed to marry your brother. If people in town caught wind that I'd now turned my sights to you, imagine what that would do to my reputation."

The words were a punch to the gut. He might not care what anyone in Stonecreek thought about him, but it was stupid to think Maggie would feel the same way. She was the mayor after all and up for reelection in the fall. He stared at her profile for several long moments. Her hair had fallen forward so that all he could see was the tip of her nose. She didn't turn to him or offer any more of an explanation.

"I understand," he told her finally.

"I had a good time tonight," she whispered, "but us being together in Stonecreek is different."

"I get it." He made a show of checking his watch. "It's almost eleven. We should head back."

Her shoulders rose and fell with another deep breath. She turned to him and cupped his jaw in her cool fingers. "Thank you, Griffin. For tonight. I really like the man you've become." Before he could respond, she reached up and kissed his cheek.

He wanted to grab her and pull her close, prove that she couldn't ignore this spark between them. Instead, he nodded, tucked a loose strand of hair behind her ear and took his keys from the pocket of his jeans. "Do you have a curfew these days?" he asked, forcing a playful tone. He wouldn't let her see how much her tacit rejection hurt.

"I'm an adult." She gave a wry smile. "Although I texted my dad earlier to let him know I'd be late. It's strange living in the house again. Morgan and Ben were little kids when I went to college."

"It's not like you've been out of their lives for years." They made their way down the now-empty street of the quaint coastal town. "You're all close."

"True," she admitted, "but my dad has never been a real 'hands-on' parent, and I'm always busy with work. It seems like Morgan and Ben have raised themselves, and that's not the way it should be."

"Don't give yourself a hard time. I'm sure they're doing great."

"Morgan has blue hair."

He gave a mock shudder. "A harbinger of evil without a doubt."

"Point taken," she said, nudging his arm as they walked. "I'm probably overreacting. I'll chill out."

"Chill out." He chuckled. "I haven't heard anyone use that phrase for years. You're cute, Maggie May, even if you shot me down during the best nondate of my life."

He opened the SUV's door for her. "Maybe we can go on another nondate?" she suggested with a small smile as she buckled her seat belt.

Okay, not shot down entirely.

Griffin found himself smiling as he walked around the front of the Land Cruiser. He wasn't giving up on Maggie. She was right. He didn't care about her history with Trevor or what anyone in Stonecreek thought. He liked her, and it was more than physical attraction. He'd seen and done enough in life to know she was worth fighting for. Griffin was a fighter.

He hopped in the car and turned the key in the ignition. "Next time we should head up to Portland. I was there a couple of months ago, and they have some great new restaurants." When she didn't respond, he looked over. "Maggie, what's wrong?"

She was furiously tapping the screen of her phone, the scowl on her face lit by its glow. "Morgan's missing," she whispered, then lifted the phone to her ear.

Griffin pulled away from the curb, glancing in her direction every few seconds. "Since when?"

She held up a hand at the same time she said, "Hey, Dad…No, I'm on my way back. We're about an hour from town." There was a short pause. "It doesn't matter who. Tell me about Morgan…Maybe she's just late." Another pause. "Grounded for what?" She blew out a sigh. "I get it. When was the last time you checked on her?…After dinner. What time did you have dinner?" She glanced to the clock on the dashboard. "Three hours, then," she muttered. "You've called her friends? Where does she like to hang out?" Pause. "And you're sure Ben's at home?" Her free hand tapped a rapid beat against her leg. "Have him reach out to her friends. Don't call Tom yet. I'll be there as soon as I can. We'll find her, Dad."

She clicked off the phone and dropped it into her lap, her eyes squeezing shut.

"Your sister?"

"She failed Biology last semester so she's doing summer school. Dad grounded her tonight for a bad test grade."

"Maybe he's a little more clued in than you thought," Griffin suggested gently.

Maggie snorted. "Other than the fact that she went to her room after dinner and he just checked on her and she's gone."

"She sneaked out?" Griffin didn't try to hide the shock in his voice.

"Apparently." Maggie held the phone up to her ear again. "Morgan, if you get this message, call me. Call Dad. Let us know you're okay."

"She's okay." Griffin reached across the console to pat her leg.

"How do you know?"

"Didn't you used to sneak out at night?" He felt his eyes widen. "Wait. You never sneaked out?"

"Not once. Why would Morgan sneak out? She barely has rules as it is."

"Um, she was grounded for a test grade. That's something."

"One night," Maggie countered. "Couldn't she have stayed in for one night?"

"Who are her friends?"

"I don't know anymore." Maggie thumped the heel of her hand against her forehead. "My dad doesn't know. He doesn't remember names or ask questions." She sighed. "I have a feeling they're wild."

Griffin thought about that for a moment, then nodded. "I have an idea. We'll find her, Maggie. Don't worry."

She looked over at him, the lights from the highway casting her pale skin in and out of shadow. "You can drop me off downtown. My car's parked there. This isn't your problem."

"Haven't you heard?" he asked with a small half smile. "I'm working on my hero status now that I'm back in town."

Chapter Nine

Maggie clutched her hands together as Griffin headed down the dark road toward the address he'd been given over the phone. They were about thirty minutes east of Stonecreek, in a section of ranch land she rarely visited.

According to what Griffin had been able to discern from a friend's nephew, there was a big party happening in one of the fields out this way. If Morgan had been looking for trouble, this was the place for it.

"We'll find her," he said for what must have been the tenth time since they'd begun to search. Morgan still wasn't picking up her phone and she'd disabled the location service built into it.

If Griffin wanted the role of hero, Maggie had no problem seeing him like that. Although, it was still difficult for her to believe Griffin Stone would take time out of his night—even a minute—to help track down her wayward sister.

Suddenly, he hit the brake as a figure stepped out onto the road, waving frantically.

"It's Cole Maren, the kid who's been working with me on the tasting room." Griffin pulled onto the gravel shoulder, his headlights illuminating the beat-up Chevy and a smaller silhouette sitting in the back of the truck bed.

"Morgan," Maggie breathed, heart hammering in her chest. All the anonymous faces she'd ignored on the side of milk cartons and in the post office ran through her mind as relief bubbled up inside her. She sent out a silent prayer for every missing child to be found safe as Morgan shielded her eyes against the glare of the light.

Griffin threw the truck into Park and jumped out. "What the hell?" He stalked forward with Maggie following.

"Morgan, are you okay?" she called as she rushed toward her sister.

"Is that you, Maggie?"

"I trusted you. I gave you a chance." Griffin grabbed the lanky boy by the shirt, yanking him forward, then slamming him into the side of the truck. "What did you do to her?"

As shocked as she was by Griffin's treatment of Cole, Maggie's first concern was Morgan. She reached her sister, who brushed away her touch. "I'm fine, Mags. Tell me Dad doesn't know I'm gone."

"Let me go," Cole shouted. "I didn't do anything wrong."

"Hey, stop that." Morgan jumped off the back of the truck, stumbling once before righting herself. Maggie felt sick to her stomach. Clearly, her sister had been drinking or worse. "You're going to hurt him."

"That's right." Griffin glanced at Morgan, then back to Cole. "For every way you hurt her, I'm going to hurt you."

"He hasn't done anything," Morgan screamed when Griffin tightened his grip on the teenager, who looked defiant but wasn't fighting Griffin's hold.

"Griffin, it's okay." Maggie made her voice soothing. "Let him go."

"I gave you a chance," Griffin repeated, shoving away from the boy and walking toward the back of the truck. His fists were tightly clenched at his sides.

Morgan placed a hand on Cole's arm, but he shrugged away.

"Where have you been?" Maggie stepped between her sister and Cole. "Why haven't you answered any calls or texts?"

"Check your phone," Morgan said unapologetically. "There's no service out here."

"You were grounded."

"For failing a stupid summer school science test," Morgan whined. "Which is your fault anyway."

"How am I to blame for a bad grade in science?"

Morgan snorted. "It's your fault I'm grounded," she clarified. "Dad didn't pay attention to any of my grades until you gave him grief about needing to be more involved. Suddenly, he decides to check up on me the weekend of the most important party of the summer."

Cole let out a harsh laugh at that. "The party was stupid."

"Then why did you come out here?" Morgan asked, her tone accusing.

"I don't know," Cole shot back, throwing up his

hands, "but it sure wasn't to get in trouble for pulling you out of there. I should have just left you to it."

"You said they called the cops."

"I'm sure someone was going to. And you've been drinking."

"Morgan," Maggie gasped, unable to contain her disappointment even though she'd guessed as much.

Morgan ignored Maggie and stepped around her to point a finger at Cole. "You drink. I've seen you drink."

"Not tonight." He looked past Morgan toward Maggie. "I promise I'm not drinking and driving."

Maggie nodded. "Thanks for taking care of Morgan." She didn't know Cole, although everyone was familiar with Toby Maren's drunken antics. But she could see how upset the kid was by this situation and her sister's involvement in it.

"He didn't take care of me," Morgan insisted, whirling on Maggie. "I don't need anyone to take care of me. I'm fine on my own."

"Not hanging all over Zach Bryant," Cole said, crossing his arms over his chest. "He's a loser, Morgan."

"At least he *likes* me." Morgan patted an angry hand against her chest. "He thinks I'm hot. He said so."

Cole opened his mouth, snapped it shut again. Morgan let out a frustrated groan, and Maggie sighed.

"What happened to the truck?" Griffin asked, stepping forward.

The boy stared at Morgan for a long moment before turning his attention to Griffin. "It overheated. Stupid piece of junk. The fan belt broke."

Griffin gave a curt nod. "Get in the Land Cruiser.

I'll take everyone home, and then you and I can come back out here tomorrow and put in a new belt."

Cole snorted. "Are you going to slam me up against the truck again?"

"Not tonight," Griffin said, his mouth thinning. Maggie waited for him to say more or apologize for how he'd handled Cole, but he only turned and stalked to the SUV, calling, "Let's go," over his shoulder.

Morgan gave Maggie a look like she wanted to argue. "Now, Mo-mo," Maggie said. "As soon as you have cell service, call Dad."

"We'll be home in twenty minutes," Morgan complained.

"You'll call him first," Maggie insisted. "He's worried."

Morgan grabbed her purse from the back of Cole's truck and stalked toward the Land Cruiser. "Maybe if the town would pay for more cell phone towers, we would've been able to call for help."

"Maybe if you hadn't sneaked out in the first place, this wouldn't be an issue for any of us."

Maggie watched as Cole leaned into the driver's side and grabbed his phone and wallet. "Thank you again," she said, moving in step next to him. "She'll appreciate it someday."

He shrugged. "Apparently, I didn't do anything but make her mad."

"You were her friend."

"She's really smart at school," Cole said with a shrug, "so I don't know why she wants to hang out with the people I do. We're not good enough for her."

Maggie put a hand on the kid's arm, waiting until

he turned to look at her before speaking. "Don't say that about yourself," she told him.

Cole rolled his eyes. "You know who I am, right? My dad and brother and the fact that my mom took off years ago."

"All circumstances you can't control."

"Yeah," he agreed after a moment. "But I've done plenty of bad shi—" He broke off and gave a small shake of his head. "Your sister should not be hanging with us."

The utter conviction in his words broke Maggie's heart. Everything was so clear in her world—who she was and her place in the community. It embarrassed her to realize that even after two years serving as mayor she didn't have a clear understanding of how people might be falling through the cracks in her town.

"Are you two coming or what?" Griffin called from the SUV.

"I'm still grateful," Maggie told Cole as they started walking again.

She climbed in, and Griffin turned back the way they'd driven on the highway. No one spoke, and Maggie eventually flipped on the radio, hoping the noise would disguise the tension filling the vehicle.

A few miles outside of town, her phone began to ding, and she could hear Morgan's making the same kind of incessant chirping.

"Text Dad," she commanded, looking around her seat to make certain her sister complied.

"I've got twenty-four missed calls from him," Morgan murmured, and Maggie thought she detected a slight note of wonder in her sister's voice.

"He was worried." Maggie looked at Cole. "Is there anyone you need to call?"

The boy's lips formed an almost painful smile. He pulled his phone from his back pocket and held it up, the screen resolutely dark. "No one's worried about me."

"Oh," Maggie breathed. She turned toward the front again, glancing at the hard set of Griffin's features. "Thanks for helping me track her down."

He nodded. "Cole, you guys still out on Maple Lane?"

"Yeah, but you can let me off wherever. I'll walk."

Griffin made a noise that was somewhere between a snort and a sigh. "I'm taking you home."

He turned off the highway onto a dirt road, driving past ramshackle houses and a few trailers thrown into the mix. Maggie knew this part of town existed, but she wasn't familiar with it. Another strike against her as mayor, she supposed.

"Dad says I'm grounded for the whole summer," Morgan complained from the back seat. "Why did he have to start caring tonight?"

"He's always cared," Maggie told her, "but he gets distracted."

"It's not fair," her sister insisted. "I only wanted to—"

"This is it," Cole announced.

Maggie heard Morgan's tiny gasp and tried hard to hide her own reaction to the property in front of them. The house—if you could call it that—was little more than a dilapidated double-wide trailer with boards covering one of the windows and a tarp draped over half the roof. The yard was riddled with weeds and various broken lawn chairs strewed about. It was difficult to see how bad it truly was with only the headlights illuminating a narrow swath across the property as Griffin pulled into the gravel driveway. The Land Cruiser dipped as it hit a rut and Griffin steered toward the edge of the drive.

"I'll get out here," Cole said, his voice tight. "If the dogs start barking, my dad will wake up."

Griffin stopped and put the truck into Park. "You'll be okay?" he asked, eyes trained on the ramshackle house.

Cole laughed. "I'm fine." He opened the door to climb out, and Maggie reached behind her seat to slap her sister's knee.

"Thanks for your help tonight," Morgan mumbled.

"Seems like I did more harm than good," Cole said with another hollow laugh. "What's new?"

He slammed the door shut and started up the driveway, a dark silhouette in the glare of the headlights.

Griffin watched him for a moment, then thumped his closed fist on the steering wheel. A moment later he got out and jogged toward Cole.

"Griffin Stone's kind of intense," Morgan said, shifting forward and resting her chin on the back of Maggie's seat.

"How does he know Cole?" Maggie asked, wondering what they were talking about in the driveway.

"Cole works at Harvest." Morgan blew out a breath. "He hates me."

"He doesn't hate you." Maggie shifted so she could look at her sister. "He was trying to keep you safe tonight."

"He thinks I don't belong with his friends. Like I'm such a loser I can't fit in with the popular crowd."

"The way he said it to me," Maggie explained, "was that he believes you're too smart to lower yourself to the standards of kids who only care about the next party."

"No way." Morgan laughed. "Cole would never have strung so many words together in one sentence."

"More or less." Maggie raised a brow. "You get the gist."

"I can take care of myself," Morgan said through clenched teeth. "I'm not a baby."

"No one thinks you are." Maggie ran a fingertip across Morgan's forehead, along the baby-fine strands at her hairline. Morgan used to love for Maggie to play with her hair. They'd snuggle in Maggie's bed late at night in the months after their mom had died. Morgan was only five, infinitely too young for that kind of loss.

"Why were you with Griffin tonight?" Morgan asked, her voice gentler than it had been earlier. Curious but not accusatory.

"We drove down to the coast. I'd spent the whole morning at the Pioneer Day Festival and wanted to get away for a bit."

"You left a town event?" One side of Morgan's mouth curved. "First the wedding and now you're skipping out on official duties. Who's the real rebel around here?"

Maggie was saved from answering when Griffin returned to the car.

"Everything okay with Cole?"

"He didn't do anything wrong," Morgan offered

from the back seat. "You don't need to be so hard on him."

"He told me he wants to change his reputation," Griffin said, shifting the SUV into Reverse. "So he should stay away from parties where the cops are going to be called."

"He was only there for a few minutes," Morgan argued. "He came in, pulled me out and we left."

Griffin flicked a pointed look at Maggie. "He mentioned that."

"Morgan, no more sneaking out."

"Tell Dad not to ground me."

"I can't." Maggie sighed. "He's the parent, and he's trying. Give him a little credit."

"It was one stupid test and she didn't give us a decent study guide. I don't even know if I'm going to go to college."

Maggie sat forward so abruptly the seat belt cut into the skin at the base of her neck. "Excuse me?"

"Just because it was your path," Morgan said, derision dripping from her voice, "doesn't mean it's mine. Ask Grammy. She'll be happy to tell you all the ways I pale in comparison to you. I have to find my own way."

"Okay," Maggie said slowly, ignoring the way her stomach lurched. They reached her father's house, and Griffin pulled into the driveway. "We can talk about that later. Go deal with Dad."

"Fine." Morgan gave another put-upon sigh. "Are you coming in?"

"Give me a minute."

"Thanks for the ride," she said to Griffin.

"You're welcome."

She opened the door and started to climb out. Then

she scooted back over to the center of the back seat. "Tonight wasn't Cole's fault. For real. Don't...like... fire him or anything, okay?"

Griffin nodded. "He still has a job at Harvest."

When Morgan closed the door, Maggie dropped her head into her hands. "What happened to our perfect night?"

"Too much adulting," Griffin said, reaching out to massage his fingers against the back of her neck.

"She's out of control," Maggie whispered.

"Only by your standards. In normal teenager land, she's doing great."

Maggie snorted. "Not go to college? Are you joking?"

"I didn't make it to college," Griffin reminded her.

"You're different. Do you think Morgan is going to join the army with her current path?"

"She's got nothing on me as a teen," Griffin answered immediately. "Probably not on Cole Maren, either."

"You were hard on him." Maggie undid her seat belt, rested a hand on Griffin's arm. He stiffened under her touch. "Why?"

He didn't answer for a moment, only lifted his hands in front of him like the answers to all of life's questions could be found in the lines on his palms.

"I know he comes from a troubled family," she continued. "But he seems like a good kid."

"He reminds me of me at that age, and that's not saying much." Griffin squeezed his hands into fists. "Would you have dated me when we were younger?" He laughed. "Don't answer that. You won't date me now, so there's no way I would have stood a chance back then."

She felt her mouth drop open. "You wouldn't have wanted a chance when we were in high school. I was three years younger for one thing, and not at all your type for another. Now is different. It's not about you, Griffin. You don't understand how things are in this town."

"An excuse and we both know it."

Maggie reached for the door, then stopped. Was he right? Was she using her position as mayor as a reason not to take a chance with Griffin? What would be so bad if she and Griffin were dating? Everyone thought she was horrible for walking away from her wedding and Trevor. How much worse could her reputation get at this point?

She realized with sudden clarity that her reputation was not the issue. She'd learned a painfully abrupt lesson in the past week. People would judge her no matter what, and she was sick of caring about the opinion of everyone around her. But what she did care about was having her heart well and truly broken.

Walking away from Trevor and taking the blame for ruining the wedding had been humiliating—but also brought a strange kind of relief. Griffin would be different. He was a man who truly had the ability to hurt her if she gave him the chance.

Could she trust him?

"I'm scared," she whispered, then blew out a breath as he took her hand in his. "I haven't been truly terrified of something for years."

"I'm not going to hurt you," he said like he could read her mind.

She turned to him, gazed into his green eyes, lit
by the dashboard lights. The mix of vulnerability and
hope there made her heart hammer in her chest. Griffin
didn't let people in easily, and the fact that he seemed
ready to lower his walls for her made her want to be
brave for him in return.

"What if *I* hurt *you*?" she asked, her voice breathless.

He lifted her hand to his mouth, pressed a gentle
kiss on each of her knuckles. Her skin tingled where
his lips touched her. She wanted more. So much more.
"I'll risk it."

Risk. That was the key word. There was no good
return without taking a risk.

Maggie licked her lips, then leaned over and kissed
Griffin. His mouth was soft yet firm against hers. She
breathed in the scent of him, clean and spicy, and realized that everything about this moment felt right. Despite the crazy circumstances that led them here, she
couldn't imagine being with anyone else in the world
right now.

Griffin tilted his head, and she opened for him as
he deepened the kiss. A moan rose in her throat, or
maybe the sound came from him. It was difficult to
know where she left off and he began. Her body was
on fire, and she tried to move closer, wanting the feel
of his body against hers. Wanting everything he could
give her.

But the blasted man was in no hurry. He seemed
content to savor her, trailing kisses across her jaw and
nipping on her sensitive earlobe. She gave a little cry in
response, and desire pooled low in her belly. Her body

was alive in a way she'd never experienced. Griffin's kiss was everything.

He cupped her face in his hands, kissed her once more, then pulled away.

She shook her head, twining her arms around his neck. "Not enough," she whispered.

"Not nearly enough," he agreed but pulled away farther, circling her wrists with his fingers. "But we're in the driveway of your father's house. Anyone could walk by and see us."

She rolled her eyes. "It's after midnight."

"Your dad could come out."

"We're adults, Griffin. I'm not the one who was grounded tonight."

"I want to be respectful."

"Words I never expected to hear coming from you," she said with a laugh.

He smoothed his thumbs over the pulse points on the insides of her wrists, the touch at once tender and erotic. "I told you I've changed."

"Thank you again for tonight, both the date—" she emphasized the word, needing to reassure herself it was real "—and your help with tracking down Morgan."

"You're welcome," he told her. He glanced past her toward the house, his mouth quirking on one side. "Your dad is headed this way."

Maggie tugged her arms out of his grasp and automatically smoothed a hand through her hair. She opened the SUV's door just as her father reached the car.

"Everything okay?" he asked, glancing from her to Griffin with a raised brow. "Hey, Grif."

"Jim."

"It's fine." Maggie climbed out of the car.

"You two were out to dinner tonight?" Her father rubbed a hand over his face in a gesture that must have been universal for exasperated dads everywhere.

"We drove over to Lychen," Maggie told him. "I needed to get out of town."

Her father looked shocked. "That's a first. I didn't realize the two of you were friends."

"Thanks again, Griffin," Maggie said and quickly shut the door before her father could ask any questions. They stood in silence as Griffin pulled away, the red taillights disappearing around the corner at the end of the street.

"So, Griffin Stone," her dad murmured. "Seems like I'm too out of touch with both my daughters."

"You're doing fine," Maggie said, linking her arm with his. "Is Morgan in bed?"

Jim sighed and let her lead him back toward the house. "I took away her phone, so now she really hates me."

"I think that's normal at her age."

He held the front door for her. "You were never like that," he said as she passed through.

"I wasn't normal," she admitted.

"You didn't get to be because of your mom," he said quietly. "I'm sorry for that."

She turned and hugged him. "You did the best you could."

"You're sweet but we both know that's not true. I'm trying to do better now."

"Good." She pulled away. "I'm going up to bed."

"Do you want to talk about you and Griffin kissing in the driveway?"

Heat colored her cheeks and she shook her head. "Nope."

"I'll admit," her dad said with a laugh, "that's a relief. But I'm here if you need me. I love you, Mags."

"You, too, Dad." She walked up the stairs, and although everything in her life was uncertain at the moment, she felt more at peace than she had in ages.

Chapter Ten

The following Wednesday morning Griffin looked up from the piece of trim he'd just cut to find Trevor glaring at him.

"Come to lend a hand?" he asked, gesturing to the men lifting load-bearing wall beams into place. Marcus had lent him several laborers to help with demolition earlier in the week, and Griffin had hired a framing crew to handle the main structure.

It was too soon to make real predictions, but if work continued at this pace they'd have the tasting room open for the busy fall tourist season. With the valley painted in Mother Nature's finest palette and the lingering warm daytime temperatures and crisp nights, Stonecreek was always a popular destination in late September and early October.

"What are you doing with Maggie?" Trevor demanded, his gaze laser focused on Griffin.

Griffin set down the circular saw he'd been using, peeled off his leather gloves and wiped a hand over the sweat beading at his temple. "I don't suppose none of your business would suffice as an answer?"

"Half a dozen people have called or texted me to say that they saw the two of you together the past week looking quite chummy."

"Um…" Griffin tapped a finger on his chin. "I don't think of Maggie as a 'chum,' but whatever works for you, Trev."

"Nothing about this works for me," Trevor shouted, then closed his eyes and took an audible breath as the men working on the other side of the room stopped to stare.

"Let's walk outside," Griffin offered, not wanting to have this conversation with an audience. He didn't particularly care about Trevor's temper, but there was no doubt the Stone brothers arguing over Maggie Spencer would be hot news. Griffin wanted to avoid anything that might upset her.

This worrying about someone else's feelings was a new thing for him. Sure he'd cared about his army buddies. He would have gladly taken a bullet for any of them. Since retiring from the service, he'd made friends on construction sites across the Pacific Northwest. But Maggie was different. He didn't want anything to give her a reason to end what was happening between them.

He'd seen her only twice since their trip to Lychen— once for a quick dinner at the pizza place in town and then a picnic and hiking at Strouds Run State Park last night. The picnic had been her idea, mostly due to the attention they'd received in town. They'd taken a long walk through the park's trail system, then spread a blanket in a grassy meadow for a romantic dinner. But it wasn't enough for Griffin.

He wanted to spend more time together—he could imagine sharing every little thing that happened in his day with her. Another new phenomenon since he'd always thought of himself as a loner. But they'd talked on the phone each night, and just hearing her voice made him happy.

The exact opposite of how he felt facing his brother now.

"I thought your lunch was a coincidence," Trevor said, hands on his hips.

"It was."

"What about this week?"

Griffin shrugged. "Not a coincidence."

"So you're taking on my sloppy seconds?"

The words were no sooner out of Trevor's mouth than Griffin reached out and grabbed his brother's shirtfront, yanking him closer. "Don't talk about her that way. You said she didn't make you happy. Why does it bother you if I'm dating her?"

"Dating." Trevor jerked out of Griffin's hold. "Why doesn't it bother you that I had her first? Unless you're seriously trying to imitate my life."

"I won't do this with you anymore," Griffin answered, even though he wanted to go after Trevor with every fiber of his being. This is how it had always started with the two of them. Trevor goading Griffin into a reaction, and Griffin taking the bait every time. Then he'd be the one to look like the hot-tempered jerk for arguing or fighting or doing something stupid.

"What if I'd married her?" Trevor straightened the

collar of his shirt, color creeping up his neck. "Would you be lusting after my wife?"

"You *didn't* marry her."

A muscle ticked in Trevor's jaw. "This is going to hurt her chances for reelection. This town is everything to the Spencers."

"It won't," Griffin insisted, even though he had a suspicion Trevor was right. Their cousin Jason had called yesterday to simultaneously warn him away from Maggie and thank him for helping to cast more of a shadow on her reputation.

As much as he wanted to believe her personal life wouldn't have an effect on the community supporting her in the election, he wasn't that naive. Emotions always played a part in politics, and those in Stonecreek were running high against Maggie.

"Whatever you're playing at with her can't last," Trevor said, his tone cool.

Griffin kept his features placid, even though he felt his brother's words like a sharp right to the jaw.

"It's none of your business," Griffin muttered, hating that it was the best he could come up with. He wasn't one for long relationships, hadn't had a girlfriend for more than a few months at a time his whole life.

Yes, Maggie was different, but had he really changed that much?

"You already realize it." Trevor's smile was smug. "I knew this was some stupid game to get back at me."

"For what?" Griffin demanded, letting anger seep into his tone. "I left Stonecreek. I have a life beyond the family business. I got out from under Dad's thumb. Why would I want to get back at you?"

The smile vanished from Trevor's face as quickly as it had appeared. "Because he loved me," he answered before turning and walking away. He climbed into his Porsche and raced down the driveway, disappearing in a cloud of dust.

Bile rose in Griffin's throat, razor sharp and rancid. He swallowed against it, then paced to the edge of the hillside. Since he'd returned home, the vineyard felt like a sanctuary. He walked the rows of vines in the early mornings, sometimes on his own or sometimes with Marcus, who kept the same presunrise hours as Griffin did.

He loved the scent of the earth and watching the grapes begin to flower, the young shoots like buttons on the tips of the vines. He and Marcus spoke about the growing cycle, the climate, pests and the season's progression to the fruit set and beyond to harvesting. It calmed Griffin in a way nothing had in years to reconnect with the land that way.

In the space of a few minutes Trevor made him question everything about his life here. Were he and Maggie doomed from the start? Was he only trying to prove that his dad had been wrong about him for so many years? Was all of this a mistake?

He turned back to the tasting room, watching as workers made their ways in and out of the front of the building. It had seemed so easy—returning and becoming part of the business again. Marcus sought him out each day, asking his opinion on various viticultural practices. It was what Griffin had wanted growing up—to become an integral part of Harvest. Trevor's words reminded him he was an outsider even now.

Then Maggie appeared from around the corner, her gaze taking in the busy construction site as she walked.

She wore a fitted dress that just grazed her knees with a wide belt encircling her waist. Her hair was pulled back in a low ponytail, and his fingers itched to pull out the elastic that held it in place and watch it cascade over her shoulders. What he wanted more was to see it pool across his pillow, but he was determined to take things slow. She was skittish and he didn't want his shocking need for her to ruin things before they started.

Griffin had never considered himself much of a gentleman, but for her he wanted to make everything perfect.

He held up a hand and waved when she looked in his direction, and the smile that lit her face made his heart stammer.

He wanted to be a man who always deserved that smile.

"Hi," she said, her grin turning shy as she approached him. "I hope you don't mind a surprise visit." She glanced around, then reached up and brushed a quick, nervous kiss across his lips.

He felt the touch all the way to his toes.

"I'm always happy to see you." He wrapped his arms around her waist and pulled her close, chuckling when a couple of wolf whistles came from the men taking a break for lunch. "But I didn't think you were comfortable coming out here."

"I'm not," she admitted, her cheek resting against his chest. "I parked at the office and walked over here so I could hide in the trees if I saw your mom or Trevor."

"You don't need to hide from anyone." He dropped a kiss on the top of her head. "Especially not my mom."

"Liar," she whispered. "But thank you for saying that."

There was a note of sadness in her voice that made pain slice across his chest. "What's wrong?"

"Nothing."

He cupped her face in his palms and tipped up her head until she met his gaze. Tears swam in her eyes. "Liar," he said softly, swiping his thumbs across her cheeks.

She sniffed and flashed him a watery smile. "Is there someplace we could go and talk?" She looked over her shoulder. "Somewhere a little more private?"

He took her hand and led her down the flagstone staircase toward the vineyard. Soon they were surrounded on all sides by vines, with only the fertile earth below them and the cloudless sky above. It was like a maze, although Griffin knew his way through the rows of grapes as well as he knew his own smile.

As much as he resented his dad for withholding love from him for so many years, he could still appreciate what Dave Stone had built.

In the fields, more than any other place on earth, Griffin understood the meaning of the word *legacy*. He glanced down at Maggie, smiled at the look on her face—pure wonder. It was a gift to share this with her, and he could tell she appreciated it. He wouldn't give her up without a fight.

"Tell me you're not breaking up with me," he said, skimming his fingers over the grape leaves as they walked. "We've only been on three official dates, and I don't think lunch counts. We haven't gotten to the good stuff yet." He stopped and turned to face her, bending his knees so they were at eye level. "I have a feeling that with us the good stuff is going to be great."

"My grammy came to see me today," she said, tugging her lower lip between her teeth.

Griffin straightened. "That's a mood dampener."

"No doubt," Maggie agreed.

"Trevor confronted me at the work site a few minutes before you arrived. I'm guessing they conveyed similar messages."

She sucked in a breath. "I'm glad I missed him," she admitted.

"Tell me about your grandma."

"She told me I'm tarnishing my reputation beyond repair by seeing you so quickly after…"

"Trevor gave me a similar version of the same message." Griffin turned, unable to look at her. Unwilling to know if she was walking away. He plucked a bud from a vine and rolled it between his fingers. In a couple of months, they'd be working all hours to ensure the harvest went off without a hitch. Would he still be in Stonecreek when autumn rolled around?

He couldn't imagine leaving Maggie, but it might be too difficult to stay if they weren't together.

"Why is it selfish for me to want to be happy?"

"It's not selfish, Maggie May. It's human."

He felt her at his back a moment later, the heat of her body as she encircled his waist with her arms. "I've made this town my life," she said against the fabric of his shirt. "I don't regret it, but I want more."

He held his breath, waiting for her to continue.

"I want us, Griffin. It doesn't make sense, and the timing is horrible." She laughed softly. "Honestly, up until that moment when you carried me into my house, I could have sworn I hated you."

"You and a lot of people around here."

"You're a different man now."

"Am I?" He'd thought that but every run-in with his brother left Griffin feeling like the same hothead he'd always been.

Maggie released her hold on him and he turned. "Or you're the same man," she suggested, "only better."

"I'm trying."

He reached for her and she twined her arms around his neck, their kiss lighting his body on fire.

"I want you," he whispered when he could finally stand to drag his mouth away from hers.

She made a noise of agreement, soft and sexy, and he felt it all the way to his toes.

"How sad is it," she whispered against his throat, "that we both live with our parents?"

He chuckled. "It's an issue, but we have options. I don't want to rush you or what's between us, Maggie. You're too important to me."

She tipped back her head and gazed up at the sky above them. "It feels like we're in our own little world out here. I could get used to this."

"Me, too. Unfortunately, I have to head back to the construction site. The architect is stopping by this afternoon to tweak the plans." He wished they could hide out like this forever. "I have an idea. Can you get away Saturday for the whole day?"

"There's a campaign event in the morning," she answered. "But after that I'm free."

"I'll pick you up at noon," he said, dropping a kiss

on the tip of her nose. He laced his fingers with hers again and they headed for the end of the row.

"Where are we going?"

"It's a surprise."

She groaned. "You can't keep surprising someone who's a type A control freak. I need to know what to wear."

"Something I can take off you easily," he said, squeezing her fingers.

"Oh." She giggled. "Well, that's straightforward."

He glanced down at her, inordinately proud to put a smile on her face after her mood when she'd shown up at the vineyard. "You type A people like straightforward, right?"

"I like you," she whispered and he couldn't stop himself from kissing her again.

They made it to the top of the hill and rounded the corner of the tasting room building. A line of men stood just outside the front door, a few on their phones while the rest talked among themselves. "Does everyone take lunch at the same time?" Maggie asked.

"Not usually." A man Griffin didn't recognize approached them. "Griffin Stone?"

Griffin nodded. "What can I do for you?"

The man held out a single sheet of paper. "I'm shutting you down."

"Are you joking?" Griffin took the paper, scanned it and muttered a curse. "This is totally bogus."

"The building department doesn't see it that way." The man shrugged. "You can file an appeal downtown. Have a good day."

Anger and frustration roared through Griffin. "Did

you know about this?" he demanded, waving the paper in front of Maggie.

She looked from him to the man climbing into the Prius parked at the edge of the construction site. "Know what? Who was that?"

Griffin swore again. "I got a cease and desist by order of the town council." He pushed the paper toward her. "More specifically, it comes from the office of the mayor."

Maggie skimmed the two-paragraph letter that stated the Stones couldn't rebuild on a designated historic site without approval from the Stonecreek Historical Society. She looked up at Griffin. "Did you get the permit?"

He threw up his hands. "What permit?"

"The one referenced here from the historical society."

"I pulled a construction permit," he said, working hard not to grit his teeth. "As one does for a construction project. All this historic site business is nonsense. It's my family's property." He narrowed his eyes. "Did you know?"

She shook her head. "No, and I apologize for that. But you have to suspend work until it's resolved."

"You can't be serious."

"The town has rules, Griffin. Even your family has to follow them."

"This isn't about my family." He plucked the paper out of her fingers. "Look at the list of names on the historical society letterhead. Your grandmother and her friends. She's got it in for us."

Maggie opened her mouth, then snapped it shut

again. "That's not what it's about," she insisted, but there was no fight in her tone.

He shook his head, amazed at how quickly his blissful bubble from minutes earlier had popped. "I need to make some calls. I've got subcontractors ready to go, and if this holds us up for any length of time, it's going to throw the whole schedule out of whack."

"I'm sorry, Griffin." Maggie's voice was quiet, defeated.

He took a breath, then reached out a finger and traced it down her cheek, as always marveling at the softness of her skin. "We say that to each other far too often."

She gave a barely perceptible nod.

"Can I walk you to your car?"

"I'm fine. Go deal with the letter."

"I'll talk to you soon, Maggie May."

He waited until she'd disappeared around the side of the building before pulling out his phone. No matter what Maggie said, this had something to do with his last name and Vivian Spencer's need to control everything that happened in Stonecreek.

But Griffin wasn't going to let anyone tell him what to do any longer. He'd find a way to fix this and keep construction on track, even if meant making enemies out of every person in this town.

Chapter Eleven

"I don't have time for this today, Morgan."

Maggie stalked away from the principal's office at the high school, hands clenched at her sides, shooting daggers at her sister out of the corner of her eye.

Instead of contrition, Morgan glared right back. "You didn't have to come."

"Mr. Peterson called me when he couldn't reach Dad. Was I supposed to ignore it?"

"Dad obviously did."

"He's working in the studio." Maggie threw up her hands. "You know he doesn't bring a phone out there."

Morgan snorted. "Trust me. I know. He barely remembers to change clothes when he's deep in a project. It used to be embarrassing when I'd have friends come over. Now I don't bother."

Maggie pushed open the metal door that opened to

the school's front staircase. Clouds billowed across the sky, a summer storm imminent. She closed her eyes and concentrated on breathing in and out, trying to calm her already-frayed nerves.

"Why, Mo-mo?" she asked, turning to face her sister. "Summer school's not even in session. Mr. Peterson just happened to be here. If he hadn't, the janitor who found you might have called the police."

"It was a dare," Morgan mumbled.

"A dare." Maggie shook her head. "Who would dare you to spray paint the first-floor lockers?"

"Friends."

"Who are these so-called friends?"

"You don't know them."

"With antics like that I don't want to." Maggie reached out and tugged on the end of her sister's blue braid. "Why do you hang around people like that?"

"They're fun," Morgan answered, although she didn't sound convinced at the moment.

"Then maybe they'll join you for the fun of scrubbing the girls' locker room."

"I sprayed one letter," Morgan said, a whine in her voice. "I should have to clean one locker in return."

"Nice try." Maggie headed down the steps toward her car, which was parked in front of the school. "You're grounded anyway. You weren't supposed to leave the house."

"Dad didn't notice."

"He's working," Maggie insisted. "You can't fault him for the time he spends on his sculptures."

"Whatever."

"Is this about Mom? Do you need to talk to someone?"

Morgan's eyes darkened, mimicking the charcoal sky above them. "She's been gone for eleven years. Why would this have anything to do with her?"

"Because it's still hard to lose your mom, Mo-mo. That doesn't change. I know because I miss her all the time."

"It's not her," Morgan mumbled, but Maggie didn't believe her. She loved her sister so much but had no idea how to break through the attitude she'd taken to wearing like armor. Unfortunately, she also had other issues to deal with today.

Maggie waited until Morgan had climbed into the Volkswagen Jetta and fastened her seat belt. "Well, you've earned yourself a visit with Grammy," she said, hitting the button on the door locks.

"No way," Morgan said automatically. "You're going to send me to Grammy for punishment?"

Maggie backed the car out of the parking space, then headed through the empty lot and onto the road that led to the Miriam Inn. "Lucky for you, this is my business with her. I need to stop in at the weekly historical society meeting."

"Going to polish each other's golden crowns?" Morgan asked with a snicker.

"Not exactly."

It was only five minutes to the far side of Main Street where the hotel was situated. Maggie had been almost there when she'd received the call from Principal Peterson. She'd returned to her office after leaving the vineyard, pulling up meeting records from the town's computer database. She wanted to believe the cease and desist order Griffin received hadn't been a personal vendetta, but she had a difficult time finding

any precedence for the historical society inserting itself into any past remodeling projects in town.

Mostly the group was concerned with paint colors
and preserving the Victorian-style homes that made
up the downtown area.

Interference like she'd witnessed at Harvest was
something new, and it made her temper spike to think
her grandmother might be purposely thwarting the
project that meant so much to Griffin.

She understood why Dave Stone would have applied for historic designation. He'd been in the process
of renovating the old building that housed the tasting
room, and the grants available for a historic building
would have gone a long way to fund the project.

"Are you mad at Grammy?" Morgan demanded as
Maggie pulled to the curb in front of the inn. "Or is
this still about me?"

"What?"

"To quote Ben, you look like you're ready to 'shank'
someone."

"When did this family become so bloodthirsty?"
She turned off the car, then flipped down the visor to
check her appearance. Pale skin, wide, uncertain eyes,
a slight tremble of her lips. All as expected. "You can
stay here if you want," she told Morgan. "I'll roll down
the windows so you get some fresh air."

"I'm coming with you. You look like you need
backup."

Maggie sucked in a shaky breath. "Thanks, Mo."

They entered the Miriam Inn, with its muted, taste-
ful walls and thick Aubusson carpet. A few people
in the lobby looked up and waved politely. Normally,
Maggie received a warm welcome, and the change

stung but she was getting oddly used to not being the town's golden girl. It was liberating to just be herself and not have to worry about constantly keeping her perfect mask in place.

"Mary Margaret," her grandmother called as Maggie and Morgan entered the conference room down the hall from the lobby. "How lovely of you to stop by. We were discussing the upcoming debate."

"Hey, Grammy, great to see you," Morgan muttered under her breath. "It's like I'm invisible to her."

"I see you, Morgan," Vivian said, her tone slightly sharper. "You're difficult to miss with that hair." She sniffed and turned to the other people at the table. "I don't understand trends these days."

Maggie placed a supportive hand on Morgan's arm. "Your hair is lovely."

Morgan leaned over and whispered, "I'm supposed to be giving you support."

"We're getting to that part," Maggie assured her. "I need to talk to you," she said to their grandmother, then let her gaze travel around the table. "All of you."

"Sit down, dear." Vivian patted the empty seat next to her. "Would you like tea or a brownie? We were just discussing Joellyn George's recent house project."

The man seated across the table made a dismissive sound. "She painted it a garish red, like it's some kind of brothel or whatnot."

"That's why we approved the town's official color palette last year," Vivian assured him. "Maggie signed off on it as mayor so we're well within our rights to require Joellyn to repaint the house."

"Can we talk about those awful streamers she has draped across the front porch?" Lucy Winters asked, wrinkling her nose. Lucy was a few years younger than Vivian, and liked to think of herself as edgy because her left earlobe was double pierced. Her husband was Stonecreek's leading family practice doctor, which gave her a certain amount of clout in the community. "We should demand she remove those."

Morgan rolled her eyes. "They're Tibetan prayer flags."

"They're tacky," Lucy said.

The more Maggie thought about the town and how they'd been running it in the same way since practically the beginning of time, she realized how out of touch and provincial she'd allowed things to become around here. Stonecreek wasn't Mayberry and they weren't living in the fifties. She needed to start leading based on what she knew would be right for everyone, not just the small group of civic leaders who had control fisted in their collective hand.

A group, unfortunately, led by her grandmother.

"The flags stay," Maggie said, gripping the back of the chair in front of her. "As long as Joellyn wants them hanging. What she does on her porch is none of our business."

Her grandmother raised a brow as the other members of the historical society shifted in their chairs or busied themselves with the paperwork in front of them. "This is *our* town," Vivian countered. "We have a duty to uphold the standards people expect from Stonecreek."

Maggie shook her head. "The town belongs to everyone who lives here. Diversity—even in decorating porches—is a good thing, Grammy. We want people to feel welcome here."

"The right people," Henry Simon added.

Maggie leveled a look at him and said slowly, "All people."

"Verbal shank," Morgan whispered behind her. "Nice one."

"What's this about, Maggie?"

"I'm up for reelection this year," Maggie answered. "I need to make sure I'm representing the voters to the best of my ability."

"You need to be certain," her grandma insisted, "that you aren't making additional enemies around town. I've been doing my best to shore up the holes in your reputation, dear, but you aren't making it easy."

"This isn't about my personal life."

Grammy smiled. "It's always personal."

"Which brings us to the point of my visit." Maggie inclined her head. "I heard that you delivered a cease and desist letter to Harvest Vineyards."

"I didn't deliver it personally," Grammy said sweetly.

"We had Roger from the building department take it over," Lucy offered. "Seemed more official that way."

"You have no jurisdiction over the Stones' property."

Henry raised a gnarled finger. "We do, actually. Dave Stone applied for historic status on several of the structures about a year before he died. He wanted the tax breaks and funding that the state offers."

"The tasting room was included in that," Lucy added.

"I've been out there," Maggie said. "Griffin's renovation is fixing the damage from the fire and improving the space. They'll be able to do more events and wine tours. It'll be good for the economy."

"Good for Harvest's bottom line, you mean." Vivian pulled out a three-ring binder from the stack of papers in front of her. "Jana Stone has been talking to people about hosting wedding receptions."

"So what?"

"That will directly impact the reception room here."

"There are plenty of weddings to go around," Maggie insisted.

"You don't know that. These tours and wine groups you're talking about bring revenue to Harvest, not the town."

"They use local caterers to provide food."

"Have you seen the plans for the second phase of construction at the vineyard?" Vivian opened the binder and flipped through several pages. "She wants to open a farm-to-table restaurant and a series of cottages."

"None of that is bad." Maggie turned to her sister. "Have you heard anything in this conversation that sounds dire for the town?"

Morgan made a show of pulling a stick of gum from her purse, unwrapping it and then popping it into her mouth. "It all sounds great to me."

"It will give them too much power," Vivian said, while the others at the table nodded. "Jana Stone will throw her money around like some sort of benevolent goddess but it will all be on *her* terms."

"Like the grant for the community center," Lucy said, nodding enthusiastically. "I heard she's going to rescind the money until after the election and then give it only if Jason wins."

Vivian sighed. "That's what I'm talking about. Maggie, in a town like Stonecreek and a public office like the one you hold, there is no such thing as a personal life. If the Stones want to giveth and taketh away their largesse, we need to show them there can be consequences on both sides."

"We aren't the Mayberry mafia." Maggie thumped her hand on the back of the chair, feeling like she'd entered some sort of alternate universe where her grammy was playing the part of a mafiosa. "Has anyone talked to Jana?"

The historical society members, even her grandmother, shook their heads. "Where did you hear about her rescinding the grant money?"

Lucy sat forward. "My daughter's best friend heard it from someone in her mommy-and-me group who goes to yoga class with Jason Stone's wife."

"That's like a bad game of telephone. I'll call Jana."

"You can't call Jana," Lucy said quickly. "If you call, then she'll know we've been talking about her and—"

"That will give her the upper hand," Vivian finished.

"Your logic is ridiculous," Maggie muttered.

Her grandmother pointed. "Watch your tone, young lady."

"Grammy, I'm sorry. This is silly. You need to tell Griffin he can go back to work on the tasting room."

"We have rules," Henry explained.

"You gave us this power," Vivian reminded her.

"Then I'll find a way to take it back. It's not right."

Lucy mumbled something under her breath.

"Oh, man," Morgan whispered.

Maggie leaned forward, zeroing her gaze on the petite woman. "What did you say?"

"I don't think any of this would be an issue if you'd

married Trevor." Lucy threw up her hands when Grammy groaned. "Don't act like that, Vivi. We all know it's true. Now she's cavorting with the other one and no one knows what to think."

"You don't have to *think* anything," Maggie said through clenched teeth. "It's my private life."

"The order has been delivered," her grandmother said, making it clear from her tone that this was the end of the conversation.

Maggie felt her mouth drop open. She was the mayor of Stonecreek yet here she was being dismissed like a child at the grown-up dinner table. She wanted to scream, but that wasn't done with her grandmother.

She owed Grammy respect and loved her more than words, but she wasn't going to be a puppet for anyone—even the woman who meant the most to her in the world.

"Is there something else you need from us, Maggie?"

"No," she said then turned and stalked away without another word.

That afternoon Brenna walked into the crowded coffee shop, scanning the tables until she found Maggie at one of the booths in the back.

With a deep breath, she moved forward, hands clasped tightly in front of her stomach. Maggie's text had been cryptic.

I need to see you. Cuppa Joe at 1.

Brenna hadn't hesitated. She'd left a note on her computer at the Harvest office saying she was taking a late lunch and driven toward downtown Stonecreek.

Although now she wasn't sure if meeting Maggie in such a public location was a good idea. She could have decided to publicly humiliate Brenna the way she'd been embarrassed at suddenly learning of Trevor's cheating.

Brenna shook her head. It didn't matter. As Marcus regularly reminded her, she'd made a mistake. That didn't make her a horrible person.

"Hey," she said, sliding into the booth.

"Did you order a cappuccino?" Maggie asked, scowling at Brenna's empty hands.

"I'm too nervous for caffeine," Brenna said with a shaky laugh. "I'll get something after."

"Nervous?"

"Your summons was kind of abrupt," Brenna admitted.

Maggie sighed and pressed two fingers to her temple. "I'm sorry. I'm upset, but it has nothing to do with you. I just needed a friend and…"

"You called me?" Brenna felt her mouth widen into a huge grin. "That's so great."

"That I'm upset?" Maggie asked with a wry smile.

"Stop. I'm so glad you called me. You never have to apologize for anything. After what I did—"

Maggie held up a hand. "I get that you regret not telling me, but I don't want to keep reliving that moment, okay? I feel like that day is going to haunt me for the rest of my life."

"I understand." Maybe Marcus was right and things would work out in the end. It was odd how quickly he'd become an integral part of her life. Between seeing him at the office, and the time he spent with her and Ellie, the soft-spoken vintner filled a hole in her heart she didn't even realize was there.

Now to have Maggie back… Well, Brenna couldn't remember a time she'd felt so happy. But she focused on her friend, noting Maggie's red-rimmed eyes and pasty complexion. "What's going on, sweetie?"

"Am I a pushover?" Maggie asked.

"No," Brenna answered automatically, mainly because she knew that was what her friend wanted to hear.

"Are you sure?"

Brenna thought about some of the late-night conversations she'd had with Marcus. He was always supportive when she talked about her worries and fears, but he never coddled her. Sometimes his straightforward opinion was tough to hear, but she appreciated the honesty.

"You can be," she admitted, then quickly added, "It's because you try to make everyone happy."

"Everyone but myself," Maggie said quietly. She thumped her head against the table. "How did I let this happen?"

"You haven't done anything wrong." Brenna reached out a hand to stroke the back of Maggie's head. "You're a good person. This town respects you."

"Do people think I'm a mouthpiece for my grandma or my family in general?" Maggie lifted her head, narrowing her eyes. "That the only thing I care about is advancing my family?"

"They know it's not the *only* thing you care about." Brenna broke off a corner of the scone on Maggie's plate and popped it into her mouth.

"Have the rest." Maggie pushed the plate forward. "I'm too sick of myself to eat."

"Where is this coming from? I don't think it's been a secret that you support your family. The Spencers are an institution around here. You're not a mouthpiece as much as a spokesperson."

Maggie shook her head. "I'm everyone's mayor. I'm supposed to represent *all* the town, not just my little slice of it."

"You do."

"What about the Stones?"

Brenna made a face. "That's more complicated." She plucked another bite of scone. "Is the rumor about you and Griffin true?"

"Where'd you hear it?"

"Come on. This is Stonecreek. Where haven't I heard it?"

"It's new and we've been keeping a low profile," Maggie said. "I didn't mean for it to happen."

"I know how that goes." She shook her head when Maggie blinked. "Forget I said anything. This is about you."

"Distract me. Make it about you instead."

Maggie split the remaining scone in half and took a big bite. Brenna didn't want to talk about Marcus, but Maggie seemed genuinely interested and at least she was eating.

"I've been hanging out with Marcus Sanchez a little." She raised her brows. "More like a lot."

Maggie's eyes widened, clearly in shock, before she schooled her features. "He's a great guy."

"You think he's too good for me." Brenna wiped

her hands on a napkin, the pastry sitting like a brick in her stomach.

"Not at all," Maggie said quickly, "but he's not exactly your type."

"We're friends. Nothing else has happened. We talk, and Ellie loves him."

"You've introduced him to Ellie?"

"Yes. Is that bad? I know I usually shield her from the men I'm dating…but I'm not really dating Marcus."

"But you want to," Maggie suggested.

"Like I said, he's too good for me."

"He's perfect." Maggie reached forward and took Brenna's hands. "You deserve someone like him in your life."

"You're a great mayor." Brenna squeezed her friend's fingers. "Not because of your grandma but because you're smart and hardworking and you care about this town. If you want to start doing things differently, that's your choice. No one else's."

"I've missed you," Maggie said quietly.

"Me, too."

Her phone buzzed and she quickly pulled it out of her purse. "It's Ellie's school."

"Go ahead," Maggie said, sitting back against the booth.

Brenna held the phone up to her ear and answered.

"Brenna," the voice on the other end of the line said, "it's Denise in the front office. Ellie got sick on the way to music class a few minutes ago. She's with the nurse and isn't feeling too good."

"I'll be right there," Brenna answered, already moving out of the booth. "Thanks for the call." She hit the end-call button. "I hate to cut this short but Ellie threw up at school."

"Oh, no. Poor thing. Puking at school is the worst." Maggie scooted out of the booth as well, and gave Brenna a quick hug. "I'll call you later to check on her."

"Don't doubt yourself," Brenna told her friend. "You've got this."

Maggie flashed a grateful smile. "We both do."

Brenna could only hope that was true.

Chapter Twelve

"Griffin's not here."

Maggie shielded her eyes against the afternoon sun as she approached the rustic farmhouse on the Harvest Vineyards property. The front of the home was cast in shadow, but she saw a figure rise from a chair on the far end of the porch.

"He went into town," Jana continued, "to meet with Roger at the building department and try to straighten out the mess your vindictive grandmother and her group of cronies left us in."

"I'm here to talk to *you*," Maggie said simply, deciding it best to ignore the comment about her grammy.

Jana walked to the top of the porch steps. "And which one of my sons do you want to talk about?" she asked, her tone crisp and a little tart, like the first bite of a fall apple.

"I'd like to speak to you regarding your grant for the community center."

"Ah. Of course." Jana sniffed as if she'd just taken a whiff of something unpleasant. "Priorities and all that."

Claws out, Maggie thought. Good to know going in. She and her former mother-in-law-to-be had never been particularly close. Maggie had gotten the impression Jana didn't approve of her, although she couldn't have been certain of the reason. Trevor told her she was being paranoid, and while Jana was never outright rude, she kept her distance no matter how much Maggie tried to connect with her.

Clearly, Jana no longer felt the need to keep up the pretense of civility. So be it. Maggie knew now she could deal with much worse.

"Do you have a few minutes?"

Jana inclined her head and leveled Maggie with a stare that weeks ago would have made her knees knock. Lately she'd become rather skilled at tolerating glares.

"If now doesn't work, we could set up a time next week. Either here or at my office."

"Now is fine."

Maggie followed Jana to the cozy seating area at the far end of the porch. A wrought iron love seat with thick cushions was arranged next to two wicker chairs and an iron table in the middle.

"Would you like a glass of iced tea?" Jana asked, polite but cool.

"No, thanks." Maggie lowered herself into one of the chairs as Jana took a seat on the love seat. She took a deep breath and said, "First, I wanted to apologize to you for the trouble you went through with the wine for the wedding. I'm sure you were upset that—"

"The wine is nothing," Jana interrupted with a wave of her hand, "compared to how I felt about my son being left at the altar."

"Of course," Maggie agreed automatically. Her decision to take the blame for calling off the wedding was destined to haunt her for all eternity. "I'm sorry for that, too."

"Trevor insists it wasn't your fault. Griffin is even more adamant."

Maggie kept her features schooled. "Trevor and I made the decision together."

"It's like there's something both my boys know but aren't telling me."

"I'm sorry," Maggie said slowly, trying to figure out how to avoid revealing too much, "for any pain and embarrassment this caused you. It wasn't my intention."

"Truly?" Jana asked almost absently. "Part of me wondered if the last-minute cancellation had been some overarching scheme to humiliate my family."

"No," Maggie breathed.

"I wouldn't put it past your grandmother." Jana's tone was scathing.

Maggie opened her mouth to argue, then snapped it shut again. She thought for a moment about how to answer. "I look like a heartless witch in all this. Grammy is probably as angry with me as you are."

"I doubt it," Jana said but laughed softly. "I want my son to be happy. Both of my sons."

Maggie nodded. "You're a good mother. They're lucky to have you."

"Thank you," Jana said, her tone gentler. "How are Morgan and Ben?"

"I thought they were fine," Maggie admitted with a

sigh. "Turns out raising teenagers is harder than I remember from when I was one."

"You were different, even before your mom died, but especially after. An old soul."

"I've heard that before." Maggie smiled. "I think it's another way of saying a boring fuddy-duddy."

"Not at all." Jana picked at a loose string on one of the cushions. "Your father's doing well? I don't see him around town often."

"He's working a lot lately. He gets pretty focused when he's sculpting."

"I remember," Jana agreed, and something flashed in her eyes, a mix of affection and understanding that had Maggie's brow furrowing. She didn't realize Jana Stone knew her father well enough to understand his idiosyncrasies.

"Were you and my dad friends growing up?"

"Of a sort," Jana said. "My family moved here when I was in high school. Jim was one of the first people I met." She closed her eyes for a moment, and when she opened them again all the emotion Maggie had seen moments earlier was gone. "So you'd like to talk about the money for the community center?"

Maggie swallowed. Apparently, the small talk portion of the visit had ended. "Is it true that you're thinking of rescinding the donation?"

"I wouldn't call it rescinding when I've yet to write a check."

"You made a verbal commitment."

Jana held up one finger. "Actually, Trevor suggested I make the donation. I never officially agreed."

"We had an understanding," Maggie insisted.

"Yes, you did," Jana agreed, and Maggie imagined

if the smooth, cool, slithery feel of a snake could be translated into a tone of voice, it would sound just like Jana Stone at the moment.

"So this is personal?" She worked to keep her voice neutral.

"Everything's personal, Maggie." Jana sounded a lot like her grandmother. "The truth is I was never convinced about the need for my money based on how it was going to be used. You know it's only been recently our family has had the financial resources to make a significant contribution to this community?"

Maggie nodded.

"I realize my support is a bit of a hot commodity now, but refurbishing a building that's only ten years old seems frivolous when there are services that could be enhanced. Trevor believed it was an important goodwill gesture—an olive branch between the Stones and the Spencers." She quirked a brow. "Although I'm not sure why it was ever my responsibility in the first place. I'm not trying to be difficult, but I don't think it's a good use of the funds."

"I agree," Maggie said quietly.

"You do?" Jana asked, clearly not believing the words.

"Yes," Maggie continued. "I've thought more about the project." She paused, then added, "I've been thinking about a lot of things recently that have been ignored for too long. Stonecreek has needs, but a decorating project isn't one of them. I'm mayor of the town, not a specific cross section of our residents. Did you know that over seventy percent of Stonecreek Elementary students are home alone after school?"

Jana shook her head.

"I'd like to do something real and meaningful to help our kids. A program that would bring people together, no matter their background or age or socioeconomic status."

"What did you have in mind?" Jana leaned forward, uncrossing her legs.

"A youth development program. I was thinking we could utilize the community center as a central location to provide mentoring, arts and athletic activities. Open to anyone but with an emphasis on recruiting kids who'd be without supervision otherwise."

"That isn't what your grandma had in mind."

"She's not the one who was voted mayor," Maggie countered.

Jana studied her for another moment. "True."

"I don't have the resources to do this on my own," Maggie admitted. "Either financially or in manpower. I was hoping if it appealed to you, that you'd be willing to head up a youth development committee."

"You want me in charge of it?" Jana looked incredulous.

"If you have time." Maggie nodded. "And you're interested."

"I'm interested," Jana said. "But I'm not going to jump through a bunch of bogus hoops because of my last name."

"You won't have to," Maggie promised.

"I won't be able to get started until Griffin straightens things out on the tasting room. That project needs to stay on track."

"I'll do my best to make sure it does."

They both looked up at the sound of a vehicle pulling up the driveway. Butterflies fluttered across Maggie's stomach as Griffin's Land Cruiser came into view.

"He's been happy since he came back to Stonecreek," Jana said, rising from the love seat. "Different than he was before, more at peace."

"Um, that's good." Maggie stood as well, smoothing a hand over the front of her dress.

"I think you have something to do with the change in him."

Maggie turned toward Jana. "Really?" She wasn't sure whether she was more shocked to hear the words or the fact that they were coming out of Jana's mouth.

"I don't think it comes as a surprise that I never approved of you and Trevor together."

Maggie gave a soft chuckle. "He told me I was imagining it."

"I love both my boys." Jana fingered the delicate gold chain around her neck. "I try to let them make their own decisions, even when I believe they're making a mistake."

"It would have been a mistake for Trevor and me to marry," Maggie murmured. She'd known it for some time but somehow knowing Jana agreed gave her a sense of comfort.

"You're tied to this town in a way he isn't. In a way I don't believe he wants to be, even if he doesn't see it yet. Griffin is different." She held up a hand to wave as Griffin parked and climbed out of the SUV.

Maggie mimicked the gesture, smiling at the shocked look on his face as he took in the two of them together.

"Griffin hasn't lived in Stonecreek for almost a decade," Maggie pointed out gently.

"But it's still his home." Jana placed a hand on Maggie's arm. "It always will be. He belongs here, but he needs us to help him understand that."

Maggie nodded, trying not to look as shocked as she felt. "I'll try."

"How did it go in town?" Jana asked Griffin as he walked up the porch steps.

"I spoke with the guys down at the building department." He gave his mother a quick hug, then glanced over at Maggie. "What are you doing here?"

Not exactly a warm and fuzzy greeting, but Maggie smiled anyway. "I came to see your mother."

One thick brow rose.

"We had a lovely talk," Jana said, patting his shoulder. "I have a few phone calls to make now. Email me some of your initial thoughts on the youth program, Maggie."

"I will," Maggie promised. "Thank you."

The front door clicked shut behind Jana, and Maggie met Griffin's questioning gaze with a shrug. "I'm not going to apologize again, because we say those words too often. But I will do everything I can to make sure the historical society approves your permit."

"Roger told me you'd already talked to him about how to push it through."

She nodded. "I wish I could just make it disappear but—"

"It's okay." Griffin stepped forward, laced his fingers with hers and drew her closer. "And hopefully this will be the last time I say the words for a long time, but I'm sorry, Maggie. I should have known you didn't know about the order. This isn't your fault. I'm a big boy, and I'll manage through whatever roadblocks your grandma and her geriatric posse want to throw in the way."

"You shouldn't have to," she insisted with a sigh. "I'm the mayor. This is my town now, and I have to start managing things like I believe that's true." She reached up and kissed the side of his jaw. "You're helping me do that, and I'm grateful, Griffin."

"How grateful?" He nuzzled the side of her neck, sending sparks racing along her skin.

"Grateful enough that I need to change our plans for this weekend."

He stilled. "I'm having trouble following that train of thought, and it's not because I'm distracted by how good you smell."

"It's a surprise," she told him, her voice breathless as he made a show of sniffing her neck. "But pack an overnight bag."

He pulled back, his gaze filled with banked desire as he stared down at her. "I really like the sound of that."

When the doorbell buzzed for a third time, Brenna finally managed to drag herself off the couch to answer it. She wouldn't have been able to manage moving if she hadn't been worried the sound would wake Ellie.

After a day and a half, her daughter was on the mend from her stomach bug. Ellie had eaten some soup and dry toast earlier, although Brenna couldn't say the same for herself.

She'd woken up at 2:00 a.m. last night with the same violently upset stomach that had plagued Ellie. She'd thought there was nothing worse than her daughter being sick, but the two of them feeling awful at the same time had upped the ante tenfold.

She wiped the back of her hand across her mouth as she pulled open the door.

"Brenna?"

"Oh, Lord, no," she whispered as another wave of nausea turned in her belly.

"Are you okay?" Marcus stood on the small stoop in front of her duplex, a bouquet of flowers in one hand. "I know you called in sick today, but I got worried when you didn't answer my calls or texts and—"

"I'm going to puke," she told him, then turned and rushed toward the bathroom. After the nausea subsided, she emerged, shocked to see Marcus in her kitchen, quietly unloading the dishwasher.

"You look like death warmed over," he told her, and she didn't even bat an eye. She felt worse than death at the moment. "Go to bed. I've got things under control."

"You can't be here." She tugged on the hem of her faded sweatshirt. "We're sick."

"I see that," he agreed. "Ellie told me she's feeling better. I'm going to heat up soup for her when I'm finished here."

Tears pricked the backs of Brenna's eyes, a mix of gratitude and embarrassment. She never let anyone see her unless she was showered, with her hair fixed and makeup applied.

"I'm a mom," she said weakly. "I don't need to rest."

"Go rest anyway." He moved toward her, but she backed away when he would have touched her.

"You can't see me like this." She smoothed a hand over her stringy hair, then cringed.

"Too late." His smile was tender. "Rest, Brenna. Let me help you."

She wanted to argue, to tell him that she could

handle her own life, even with a raging stomach bug. She'd learned not to depend on anyone but herself. Men like Marcus didn't want to play nursemaid. Yes, they'd gotten to know each other recently, but Brenna had made sure the house was clean, Ellie on her best behavior and everything else easy and smooth whenever he'd visited.

She didn't want to scare him off by making him think she was too much trouble. Tossing her cookies every twenty minutes would definitely fall under the category of too much trouble.

Yet Marcus didn't look scared right now. He only seemed concerned and determined to make sure she got to bed. Too tired to put up any sort of real argument, she turned and headed down the hall toward her bedroom. She stopped at Ellie's door and peeked her head in the room.

Her daughter was on the floor with her favorite coloring book.

"Sweetie, I'm going to rest for just a few minutes," Brenna said. "Is it okay if Marcus is here with you?"

Ellie nodded but didn't look up from her coloring. "We're going to play Candy Land after I have soup."

"Marcus is doing Mommy a big favor while my tummy hurts. If he needs to work or just wants to watch television, you and I can play a game later, okay?"

"He said he wants to play," Ellie answered simply.

Brenna pressed two fingers to her temple and sighed. Oh, to be young and unaware that she wasn't everyone's top priority. Had Brenna ever felt that way? She'd always had the uncomfortable awareness of being a burden to her single mother. She was proud of herself for always putting Ellie first, but she also knew it could be a heartbreaking lesson to realize not everyone felt that way.

"I know, baby," she said, keeping her voice quiet. She certainly didn't want Marcus guilted into an evening of board games. "But grown-ups sometimes have to work even when they don't want to."

Ellie paused and looked up. "Feel better, Mommy," she said, and Brenna would have laughed at being summarily dismissed if she wasn't so looking forward to collapsing in her bed.

She crawled under the sheets in the darkened room, knowing she'd only get a few minutes of rest before the next round of nausea hit.

But when she opened her eyes, light slanted through the blinds over her windows and she felt weak but no longer ill.

Yelping as she glanced at the clock on the nightstand, she stumbled from the bed and down the hall, following the scent of something sweet baking in the kitchen.

"Ellie?"

"We made muffins, Mommy," her daughter announced. "Do you want one or are you still pukey?"

"I'm so sorry," Brenna said to Marcus, who was now loading dishes from the sink into the dishwasher. Seriously, what kind of superhuman man would both load and unload the dishwasher without being asked? "Why didn't you wake me?"

He shrugged, looking almost embarrassed. "I thought you needed some rest. How are you feeling?"

"Do you want a muffin?" Ellie asked again.

"Maybe later, sweetie." Brenna bent and kissed the top of her daughter's head.

"You stayed here all night," Brenna told Marcus as if he didn't realize it.

"The couch isn't bad." His mouth curved into a half smile. "Would you like toast or soup? A glass of water?" He frowned as his gaze focused on a section of her hair. "A shower?"

"I have dried vomit on me," she muttered without raising her fingers to her head. Mortification heated her cheeks.

"A little," he confirmed. "But you look like you're feeling better."

She crossed her arms over her chest. "Less like death warmed over?"

"You were beautiful even then."

She laughed. "How are you this perfect and still single?"

He inclined his head, the sudden intensity of his dark gaze making her knees go weak. "Maybe I was waiting for you to notice me."

She swallowed, her throat raw. "I'm going to shower now," she whispered. "Probably a cold one for good measure."

He grinned like her response made him happy. Like she made him happy, even with dark circles under her eyes and puke in her hair. The thought of someone—a man—caring about her no matter what made her ridiculously happy. She wondered if she could be brave enough to trust that happiness.

Griffin slung the duffel bag over his shoulder and headed out the door of the caretaker's apartment over the barn on the Harvest property when he heard the car door slam late Saturday morning.

He wasn't sure what Maggie had planned, but he couldn't wait to spend the day, and particularly the night, with her. The rest of the week had brought a mix of frustration and promise for Griffin. The meeting with the historical society had been moved to Monday, so he'd get an answer on going forward with the tasting room project at that time.

He'd filled out paperwork and submitted an addendum to his plans detailing how the renovation fitted within the society's guidelines. Roger at the building department assured him the vote was just a formality. Maggie told him the same thing, but Griffin still didn't trust that the members of the committee, led by her grandmother, wouldn't try to stick it to him just because of his last name. No matter. Griffin was a fighter, and this was one battle he didn't plan to lose.

He'd coordinated his subcontractors and gotten them to agree to an accelerated timeline so that even with almost a week delay, he could still finish the project on time and under budget.

When he hadn't been refining his construction plans, he'd spent the past few days with Marcus Sanchez, getting caught up on the current business model and the plans for grafting a few of their most popular vines to create a new vintage. But now he was looking forward to thinking of nothing but Maggie for a while.

Instead of finding her waiting to greet him, he found Trevor leaning against his shiny black Porsche convertible, hands shoved in pockets, staring at the front of the old barn.

"Remember when Dad tried to be a goat farmer?"

The question surprised a chuckle out of Griffin. "Yeah. He bought a pair," he answered. "But Grandpa still had this place and wouldn't let him keep the goats here so Dad brought them home."

Trevor straightened, stretching his arms overhead. "I thought Mom was going to kill us when they got in through the back door."

"That you left open," Griffin reminded him. "Even though I got blamed."

"You're the one who poured them a big bowl of Frosted Flakes."

"Whatever," Griffin muttered but laughed again. "You were a suck-up."

"A skill you evidently never learned," Trevor said. "Vivian Spencer is going to fight you on the permit."

"I imagine that makes you giddy. If I can't get approval for the original building with its historic status, you get to start on your new shiny monstrosity."

"It's called progress," Trevor said.

"Why do we have to compete?" Griffin asked. "I've been talking to Marcus the past couple of days. Harvest is carving out a niche as a leader in sustainable wine making. If we grow too big too fast, we'll lose some of the control we have over best practices."

Trevor thumped a palm on his forehead. "You sound just like him. This isn't what Dad wanted, Grif. He had a vision of making Harvest the biggest player in the Pacific Northwest."

"Did he?" Griffin walked a few paces to the edge of the hillside, where he could see the original estate vineyard below, the rows neat and green in the hazy sunlight of late morning. "I know I haven't been around for a while, but the way I remember it, Dad was all about his legacy and reputation, not how many barrels we produced each year."

"It's one and the same," Trevor argued.

"We both know that's not true."

"You don't know." Trevor stalked forward until he was standing shoulder to shoulder with Griffin. "You say you don't want control, but everything has to be your way."

"I'm listening to what Marcus tells me. He's the CEO, Trevor."

Trevor snorted. "A mistake on Mom's part."

"Did you stop by to gloat about my troubles with the historical society?" Griffin asked casually. "Or was there something else?"

At that moment another car came up the gravel drive that led to the barn. Trevor's eyes narrowed at the sight of Maggie's compact Volkswagen.

He let out a harsh breath. "Believe it or not, I stopped by to see if you wanted to head out on a bike ride for the day. My gear is at Mom's, but I see you have plans."

Unfamiliar guilt ripped through Griffin. Long mountain bike rides on the nearby trails had been one of the few ways he and Trevor had bonded when they were teens. He hadn't returned to Stonecreek to make an enemy of his brother.

Trevor had hurt Maggie, but if he'd been a better man… Griffin didn't want to think about that. "How about next weekend?" he suggested.

Trevor nodded. "Yeah, next weekend."

He moved toward the Porsche just as Maggie stepped out of her car. "Hi, Trevor," she said, and Griffin heard the slight tremble in her voice. "How are you?"

"Great," Trevor answered coolly. "Never better. You?"

She shrugged. "It's been a rough couple of weeks.

I guess people only appreciate a runaway bride when Julia Roberts is playing the part."

Griffin watched emotions play across his brother's features—anger, resentment and then finally guilt. As if for a few moments Trevor had forgotten the reason Maggie walked away—the reason no one else knew and the fact that Trevor was to blame for it.

"I know it's not fair," Trevor offered.

"They'll get over it eventually," she told him, her hands gripping her keys so hard her knuckles had gone white. "I hope things won't be weird between us forever. We've been friends a long time, you know?"

"You're dating my brother," Trevor said as if that explained everything.

"You kissed another woman the morning of our wedding." Although Maggie's voice was calm, it was clear from Trevor's reaction that the words hit their mark.

"I'm sorry," he whispered, and the flash of pain in Maggie's gaze made an answering ache rise in Griffin's chest.

"I wish you would have just told me you didn't want to go through with it."

"I didn't want to disappoint you."

One side of Maggie's mouth curved. "I'm not spending time with Griffin to hurt you, Trev. We've made our choices and there are consequences for both of us."

Trevor turned so his back was fully to Griffin. "I hate seeing the two of you together," he said to Maggie. Although spoken softly, the words carried through the quiet morning.

Griffin's gut twisted as she nodded. "I know, but you'll get over it. We need you to be okay with this so that everyone else accepts it. You'll do that for me. Right?"

Trevor didn't answer for several moments and Griffin would have given anything to read his brother's expression. "Yeah, I'll get over it. We're friends, Mags. No matter what."

"I hope you two aren't going to hug it out," Griffin called, unable to stay silent any longer.

Trevor looked back over his shoulder. "It's tempting just to see your reaction."

"No, it's not," Maggie said, giving Trevor a playful slap on the arm.

"Have a good time today," Trevor told Maggie, then inclined his head toward Griffin. "Both of you."

He got in his car and backed down the driveway. Maggie waited until the Porsche disappeared down the hill before approaching Griffin. "I'm glad I had a chance to talk to him."

"That was horrible." Griffin ran a hand through his hair. "I'm sick of him playing the victim. I'd like to kick his—"

"No more about your brother." Maggie lifted onto her toes and kissed him lightly. Griffin felt the tension knotted in his shoulders release as a result. "Are you ready for the best date of your life?"

"You're confident," he murmured. "I like it."

She scrunched up her nose. "Fake it until you make it," she admitted. "I'm actually nervous that you'll be bored out of your mind."

"Never with the two of us," he assured her. There was more he wanted to say. His heart pounded against his ribs as he thought of how much Maggie had come to mean to him in such a short time. He'd never expected to feel this happy and content in Stonecreek, like he really belonged here.

So much of that had to do with the woman in front of him. She made everything better. But he couldn't reveal the depth of his emotions so soon, especially when the dust had barely settled on his brother's exit from the picture. He'd scare her off, and that was the last thing he wanted to do.

Her brows lowered as she gazed up at him. "Are you sure?" she asked quietly. "You seem different right now."

"I'm good." He picked up his duffel bag and slung it over his shoulder. "And once it's just the two of us, I'll be even better."

Chapter Thirteen

The longer Maggie drove, the more her nerves took over. A few days ago the idea to surprise Griffin with a night away had seemed perfect, but now she worried that he'd find her plan boring and stupid.

"I forgot how gorgeous this part of the state is." Griffin leaned forward to look out the front window at the old-growth forest, with branches forming an archway over the two-lane road they'd turned on about twenty minutes earlier. "But I'm curious as to what we're doing out here."

They'd driven south from Stonecreek to the Ore Creek Wilderness area, which was made up of dense forests, wide canyons and quirky spires of native rock formations.

She slowed as a mailbox came into view and she turned up a winding driveway. "We don't have to stay down here," she offered. "If you'd rather head to the city and do something more adventurous, that's fine, too."

"More adventurous than what?" he asked with a soft laugh. "Remember, I don't know where we're headed."

"Here." Maggie pointed to the rustic cabin situated in a clearing ahead of them. She pulled to a stop in the gravel driveway but left the car running. "The property belongs to the family of one of my college roommates. We used to come down here on weekends to chill. I called and asked her if I could use it for the night." She gave him a hopeful smile. "I thought we could both use some time away."

"Is that a lake in the back?"

Maggie nodded. "There's a dock with canoes and hiking trails. They have twenty acres so the nearest neighbor is on the other side of the water. But there's no internet or cell service. They don't even have a TV, unless something's changed from the last time I was here. Clearly, I was a loser even in college, because while other people were at frat parties or the bars, we'd come here and play Scrabble all weekend. You probably expected something exciting like skydiving or—"

"I love Scrabble," Griffin said.

Maggie felt her smile widen. "No way. You're saying that to make me feel better."

"I once won with the word *umiak*." He spelled out the letters for her and she laughed.

"That's not a real word."

"Look it up." He arched a brow, looking wholly self-satisfied. "It's an Eskimo canoe."

"The former bad boy of Stonecreek is now a word

nerd?" Delight rushed through her as pink tinged his cheeks. "You're blushing."

"I'm not blushing." Griffin scoffed. "I don't blush."

"But—"

He pressed one finger to her lips, the touch warm and gentle. "We had an unofficial Scrabble club at one of the bases. So I'm a manly man who happens to appreciate Scrabble strategy." He leaned over the console and replaced his finger with his mouth, the kiss long and sweet like he had all the time in the world to savor her. Maybe not all the time, but all day and night, which, to Maggie, was a wonderful thing.

"It's okay that my big surprise is a quiet night at a remote cabin?"

"Sweetheart," he whispered against her lips, "the only person I want to see is you so this is perfect."

She gave a little squeal of happiness. Now that she knew he was on board with her plan, Maggie couldn't wait to show him around the property.

"What should we do first?" she asked, pulling the keys out of the ignition. "We could hike or take out the canoes. They keep fishing poles in the shed out back and there used to be a hammock between two fir trees overlooking the water." She clapped her hands. "What are you most interested in?"

"You," Griffin said, his voice a low rumble.

Her hands stilled as awareness tingled through her. "I'm still a loser even as a grown woman," she said and sighed. "This is a romantic night away. I should be more interested in getting down and dirty than going fishing. I'm sorry."

"No apologies," he reminded her. "I want to do

whatever makes you happy, although I'll admit I'm plenty interested in down and dirty."

"Me, too," she said in a squeak of breath.

He raised a brow. "More important, I want to spend time with you. And I really want to watch you bait a hook."

"I picked up a container of night crawlers." She climbed out and gave him an exaggerated wink over the hood when he got out, too. "How's that for down and dirty?"

"It's about the sexiest fishing talk I've ever heard."

"Then fishing is first on the agenda."

They unloaded the back of her car, and she showed him around the cozy cabin, unchanged from the last time she'd visited.

The walls were paneled with rough pine, and the artwork consisted of photos of the nearby waterfalls or drawings of wildlife. She'd loved this place when she and her college roommate had stayed here, and her appreciation of it hadn't waned.

"I never really took you for an outdoors woman," Griffin said as he set down his duffel bag and her backpack onto the overstuffed couch.

"I wasn't until I came here," she told him. "That's part of what makes it so special to me. My girlfriend lives in Bend now with a husband and two kids, and her parents have retired to Arizona but they still keep the place. She doesn't make it here often, but she likes it to be in use." She shrugged. "Everyone knows me in Stonecreek, so when I want to get away, I come here."

"Did you bring Trevor?" he asked.

"No," she admitted. "He was more a 'getaway to

the Four Seasons' type of guy. No one knows about this place but you."

"Not even your family?"

She shook her head. "It was easier to tell them I was going to visit my girlfriend and her family on the weekends I came here. They wouldn't understand that I needed time alone."

"I do."

She smiled. "I know, but I'm happy to not be alone this weekend. I need to unpack the groceries before we head out. Will you grab the fishing poles from the shed and I'll meet you down by the lake?"

Griffin studied her for several long moments. "Thank you for sharing this with me."

"Thanks for being the kind of guy who can appreciate it."

He grinned, then headed out the back. Maggie watched him walk toward the shed, the warm summer sun glinting off the glassy water of the lake. How had Griffin Stone become such an important part of her life so quickly? It was difficult to fathom, but there was no denying the hold he had on her heart.

It still worried her that she was headed toward heartbreak. Griffin hadn't mentioned his plans beyond the completion of the tasting room. For all Maggie knew he'd finish the work and be on his way again. Her chest tightened at the thought, but she wasn't ready to ask him outright.

Not today anyway. This was about a perfect getaway, and she was going to enjoy every second of it. She quickly unpacked the supplies, grabbed the box of worms and then followed the flagstone path that led to the lake.

Griffin met her there, a fishing pole in each hand, and for the next hour they fished and talked and enjoyed a beautiful summer day surrounded by nature.

"I give up," he said after Maggie reeled in her eighth fish. "You can outfish me and you look a helluva lot sexier doing it."

Maggie laughed as she tossed the cutthroat trout back into the water. The fish was immobile for a few seconds, then twisted and swam off to join his buddies in the depths of the lake. She wiped her hands on her jeans and made a face at Griffin. "There's nothing sexy about fishing."

"From where I'm standing there most certainly is," he said, leaning his rod against a nearby tree. She handed him her pole, then he laced his fingers with hers and tugged her closer.

"I have fish guts on me." Her words faded into a sigh as he claimed her mouth.

A few moments of kissing, and she was lost in a haze of desire. Griffin nuzzled her neck, and she bit back a moan. His arms twined around her waist, and one hand skimmed along her hip, lighting her skin on fire as it moved.

"Canoeing's next on the list," she said breathlessly, tugging away from his embrace. If he kept touching her like that she was going to rip off his T-shirt and shorts and have her merry way with him on the spot.

His chest rose and fell in uneven breaths, and it made her girlie parts want to break into a tap dance to think that he was as affected by her as she was by him.

"You're definitely focused." He scrubbed a hand along his jaw. "No wonder they elected you mayor. If you do your job with as much efficiency as you spend your downtime…"

She inclined her head, suddenly feeling far too serious. "I was elected because my grandmother told people to vote for me."

"I don't believe that for a minute," Griffin said with a frown. "I've seen you in action, Maggie. I know how much you care about the community."

"I was twenty-five during my first campaign. I had history in the town, but not much in the way of leadership experience. Grammy was determined that I'd be her successor. I didn't even want to run at first. She convinced me I could do it because I'd have her to mentor me along the way."

"Maybe that's how it started…" Griffin took a step closer.

"Nepotism," Maggie muttered. "It started as nepotism."

"You got the votes and you've earned your place in the community. This next election is all you."

She turned and looked out over the clear water. She didn't want reality to intrude on their time in this magical place. It would be waiting for her when she returned to Stonecreek whether she liked it or not.

"I saw the canoe hanging in the shed," Griffin said as if he understood she couldn't talk any more about the election or real life.

They carried the canoe and two paddles to the water's edge. Maggie took off her shoes and rolled up the cuffs of her jeans to her knees, then gasped as she waded into the cold water to climb into the front.

Griffin followed, and they paddled toward the center of the lake, the warm breeze blowing her hair as the water rippled around them.

"I love it here," she whispered but caught herself before she added *I love you* out loud. She couldn't love Griffin Stone. It was too soon. Heck, she and Trevor hadn't said those words to each other until the night he'd asked her to marry him.

She hadn't even realized she felt it until he'd slipped the ring onto her finger. Looking back now, the way she'd felt might have had more to do with expectations than emotions.

"Did you ever consider not returning to Stonecreek?" Griffin asked, and Maggie paused with her paddle dipped into the water.

She glanced over her shoulder at him, then out to the thick forest surrounding the lake. "No," she answered. "It's my home."

"You can make a home wherever you are in the world," he suggested gently. "Places where the past doesn't weigh so heavily on your shoulders."

"I suppose," she agreed, "but I can't imagine living anywhere else. Don't you feel it now that you're back? There's something special about the town. It's home."

"You're the thing that's special to me," Griffin offered.

Suddenly, a fish jumped out of the water, just in front of the boat. Maggie yelped as she released her paddle, watching as it floated just out of reach. "I wasn't expecting that," she said, leaning over the side to grab it.

"Wait," Griffin warned. "You'll tip us."

"We're fine," she assured him. "The canoe is stable."

"Maggie."

"See." Her fingers curved around the paddle's handle, and she rested a hand on the canoe's side as she lifted. She straightened and turned to Griffin, working to keep her feet balanced on either side of the floor of the boat. "You said it yourself—I'm outdoorsy. I'll add more. I'm brave and strong and have no doubts about my ability to lead the town or…" She broke off as the canoe tipped precariously, then bent her knees and managed to maintain her balance.

"Sit down," Griffin said with a grin. "Tell me more about how great you are back on dry land."

"You're not the boss of me." She dipped her paddle in the water and flipped a spray of water at him. "I'm the boss of me," she called out into the clear afternoon, laughing as the truth of the words spilled over her. She raised the paddle over her head and shouted, "I'm queen of my own world."

"You're brave and strong," Griffin shouted back, "and soon to be soaking wet if you don't sit down."

Maggie stuck her tongue out at him, then turned to lower herself back to her seat. At that very moment her footing slipped and she went tumbling into the cold water with a splash.

She surfaced with a small scream, panting to regain the breath stolen from her when she hit the cold water. Swiping her soaking hair away from her face, she met Griffin's amused gaze.

"Don't say *I told you so*," she called to him, swimming toward the paddle that floated a few feet from her.

"I wouldn't dare." She watched as he tugged his T-shirt over his head, and her mouth went dry at the sight of the hard planes of his chest. "I thought you were going to capsize us, not go for a swim." He stood, then immediately dived in, his head emerging from the water a moment later. "You forgot to invite me."

"You're invited," she whispered, mesmerized by the water beading on his chiseled jaw. "But I should have warned you it's freezing here."

He swam closer, encircling her waist with one arm. "All the more reason to head to shore so we can find a creative way to warm up." He kissed her, their legs tangling under water, and as cold as her body felt, heat infused her belly.

She pressed closer, craving more, then laughed as they both began to sink. "I should concentrate on treading water," she said, pulling away reluctantly. "Maybe you should have stayed in the canoe so we wouldn't be stranded in the middle of the lake." She lifted her chin to glance toward the shore. "Are you up for a swim?"

"No need," he answered and, with another kiss, turned and swam toward the canoe. It had drifted several yards away but Griffin reached it in a few long strokes.

Muscles bulged as he expertly lifted himself up and over the side, and Maggie felt her eyes grow wide. She was pretty sure she'd look like a beached whale trying that same maneuver.

He grabbed the paddle and steered toward her. "Take my hand," he told her and a moment later he'd pulled her up and over the side. As she suspected, she landed on her belly in the middle of the canoe, then quickly righted herself. He'd already retrieved her paddle, grinning as he handed it to her.

"You planning to stay seated this time?"

She gathered her hair in her hands and wrung the

water out of it into the boat. "I think so," she said, teeth beginning to chatter.

They paddled to the shore in silence, and as grateful as Maggie was for the bright sunshine, she couldn't wait for a hot shower to truly warm her.

She hopped out as soon as they'd beached the canoe and they carried it up into the grass.

Griffin grabbed his discarded shirt and shrugged it over his head, mischief dancing in his eyes as he took in the sight of her staring at him.

"Would you rather I keep it off?"

"Yes," she blurted, then shook her head. "No. I can't exactly think with all of that—" she waved her hand toward him "—staring me in the face."

He immediately pulled the shirt back over his head. "I don't want you thinking about anything but—" he gestured to his body with a wink "—all of this."

"Good to see that a decade out in the world hasn't changed your opinion of yourself," she told him with a laugh, and he took her hand as they walked toward the house. "But right now we both need a shower."

She led him down the hall toward the bathroom, but he tugged on her fingers until she turned to face him in the narrow space. "You can go first," he told her, releasing her hand.

"I thought this was a together kind of moment," she said, confused by his sudden reluctance.

"I wasn't joking when I said I'm happy just to be hanging out with you. You don't owe me anything."

Maggie appreciated his willingness to be a gentleman, but she was long past the point of wanting that from him. "Don't tell me you're getting cold feet." She moved her hand up his body, running her fingers along the rippled muscles of his abdomen. "We're just getting to the real adventure portion of the weekend."

He sucked in a breath, his eyes darkening. "Every second with you is an adventure, Maggie May." He scooped her up, fusing his mouth to hers, and she twined her legs around his lean hips.

They continued kissing as he maneuvered them into the bathroom and turned on the shower. As steam filled the small space, she took off her shirt, then undid the button at the top of her jeans.

Griffin was already shoving down his shorts and boxers and her whole body stilled as he straightened again. She knew he had a great body but seeing him in his full glory was another thing entirely.

"Wow," she whispered and was rewarded with a slow, sexy smile from him.

"Back at you," he said and hooked one finger under the strap of her bra, tugging it over her shoulder. He moved closer, reaching around her to undo the clasp, and she was unable to do anything but try to catch her breath as the lacy fabric fell from her body.

"Wow, indeed." He dropped to his knees in front of her, and she swallowed, then let out a little moan as he pressed a kiss low on her belly, dragging her jeans and panties down over her hips as he did.

Goose bumps erupted across her skin as his calloused palms skimmed the tops of her thighs.

"You're cold," he said, straightening. He opened the glass shower door, steam billowing out, then stepped in, crooking a finger for her to follow.

Maggie wasn't even sure her legs would hold her at the moment but she managed to squeeze into the tight space behind him.

He shifted so that the water sprayed directly onto her overly sensitive skin, and she closed her eyes, letting sensation wash over her. Griffin ran the bar of soap along her body, taking his time as layers of need built with his touch, and the spray of the water rinsed her. A moment later he knelt and nudged her legs apart. She opened for him, gasping at the first touch of his mouth against her center.

"You don't mess around," she choked out and he gave a wicked chuckle that reverberated along her nerve endings.

He kissed and sucked, nipped and licked until she thought she would lose her mind. Then she did lose her mind, crying out his name as pleasure roared through her, like fireworks erupting inside her body.

Boneless with satisfaction, she pressed against the cool tile wall to keep from sinking to the floor. Griffin took his time trailing kisses up her body until he tenderly took her face in his hands.

"Warmer now?" he asked, and the intensity of his gaze made her feel bold. She reached her hand between them, cupped his hard length and raised her brows.

"Not quite," she answered and felt him grow more rigid in her hand.

With a groan, he pressed his forehead to hers. "Then let's remedy that." He skimmed his hand along her arm, encircling her wrist and tugging it away from him. "But don't make me embarrass myself by losing control too soon."

She kissed the side of his jaw. "I make you lose control?"

"Hell, yeah."

He turned off the water, stepped out of the shower

and pulled two towels from the linen closet, wrapping one around his waist and enveloping her in the second. She looked down at her pink skin peeking out the top and reveled in how amazing this day had already been.

She led him down the hall to the bedroom, cringing a little as she took in the simple quilt covering the bed and outdated furnishings. "It's not exactly five-star accommodations."

"We'll make our own stars."

"You're a romantic at heart, Griffin Stone." She dropped the towel on the braided rug as she slipped between the sheets.

"Hold that thought," he told her and disappeared down the hall. A few seconds later he reappeared, holding a condom wrapper between two fingers.

"Romantic and practical all in one." She grinned. "My type A personality loves it."

"I had a feeling," he said, letting the towel fall from his waist as he opened the wrapper and sheathed himself. She lifted the sheet so he could join her, and her heart sang as he covered her body with his.

He kissed her long and deep and she arched off the bed with pleasure when he finally entered her. They moved together, and Maggie never imagined it could be so good. It was as if their bodies had been made for each other. She let herself be lost in the moment, and when stars rained down on her minutes later, Maggie knew she'd never be the same.

Chapter Fourteen

"Work can wait until Monday."

Brenna shook her head. "Fridays at the office are the hardest to miss. If I pick up my reservation binder and the mail that's come in, I can get caught up tomorrow so I won't be behind on Monday." She flashed a smile. "Feel free to report my dedication to the boss."

"Duly noted," Marcus said with a laugh as he steered his Range Rover down the winding highway that led to Harvest Vineyards Saturday night.

He'd gone to his house to shower and change, then returned to Brenna's apartment, insisting on driving her to Harvest when he hadn't been able to convince her to rest longer. She'd bounced back from her stomach bug quickly, and Ellie was feeling much like her normal self. Brenna's neighbor was at the apartment now, staying in case Ellie woke while they were gone.

Sirens sounded in the distance, and Marcus pulled

onto the shoulder as the noise got louder and lights flashed behind the SUV.

"I wonder what's going on," Brenna murmured when a fire truck and two police cars raced by.

Marcus's brows furrowed as the red and blue lights disappeared around a bend. "Not much out this way other than farms and the vineyard."

"You don't think they were heading to Harvest?" She gripped the side door handle as Marcus accelerated, speeding along the quiet highway.

He made the turn into Harvest, and Brenna gasped as they made their way up the long gravel drive. In the distance she could clearly see the bright glow of flames through the trees that bordered the vineyard's main buildings.

"It's the tasting room building," he whispered and she could hear the dread and disbelief in his voice.

Fear spiked through her, sharp and deep, like a blade driven into her heart. If the fire reached the vines, it would be catastrophic for Harvest.

"What could have caused it?"

Marcus shook his head. "I don't know." He slammed on the brakes, parking at the edge of the clearing. "Stay here."

Before she could respond, he was out of the car and rushing toward the burning building. Brenna lost sight of him for several seconds in the smoke, then let out a sharp cry as bright flames licked the night air.

She got out of the car, coughing when the wind shifted and smoke filled her lungs. "Marcus!" she screamed, then felt an arm wrap around her waist.

"He knows what he's doing," Jana Stone yelled into

Brenna's ear. "Marcus worked as a volunteer firefighter when he first came to Stonecreek. He can help."

Brenna nodded even though she wanted to argue. She didn't care if he'd been fire chief of the world. The thought of Marcus anywhere near that burning building made her blood run cold.

Then she looked at Jana, stark fear etched into her delicate features. Brenna hugged the older woman's shoulders. "They'll contain it. We'll rebuild."

"Again," Jana said with a strangled sob.

It seemed like a lifetime of watching the firefighters battle the blaze, but within an hour the flames subsided.

Relief poured through Brenna as Marcus, along with Trevor, walked toward them, both of their faces covered with soot and sweat.

"Did you get a hold of Griffin?" Trevor asked his mother as she broke away from Brenna to hug him.

"I've texted and left messages. He'll call when he can. Thank heavens no one was hurt." She glanced toward Marcus. "It's like déjà vu."

Marcus shook his head. "It's not a total loss. The back corner is in bad shape, but most of the building is still intact."

"Someone needs to talk to the fire chief," Trevor told Jana and Marcus. "It would be best if we were all there."

"Give me a minute," Marcus murmured.

"Of course," Jana whispered. Before leaving with Trevor, she reached out a hand to squeeze Marcus's arm. "Thank you for everything you did tonight."

"Of course." As Jana and Trevor walked away, he turned to Brenna. "Did you call the sitter and tell her we're delayed? I don't want her to worry when—"

Brenna launched herself at him, wrapping her arms tight around his neck as she kissed him. She felt him stumble back a step before he gained his footing. Then he lifted her into his arms. "I'm a mess, Brenna."

"My mess," she whispered, breathing in the smoky scent that clung to him. "Don't ever scare me like that again."

They held on to each other for several minutes. Brenna couldn't speak with all the emotions swirling through her.

Finally, Marcus set her on the ground, taking her hand between his palms. "I'm fine," he assured her. "You don't have to worry."

"I have every right to worry, stupid man." She swiped at the tears clinging to her lashes. "I'm in love with you."

His strong jaw went slack. "Say that again."

She laughed. "You heard me."

"Yes, but I want to hear you say it again."

"I love you," she whispered and leaned in to brush her lips over his.

"Is it possible I've been waiting my whole life for this moment?" he asked, smoothing a hand over her hair. "I love you, Brenna. I've loved you for so long, sweetheart. If I'd known all it would take to win you was running into a burning building, I would have found one months ago."

She gently swatted his shoulder. "It's not the burning building, and no more of that kind of talk. It's you, Marcus. You're the strongest, kindest man I've ever met and I feel like the luckiest woman on the planet that you chose me."

"I'll choose you a million times over," he whispered.

She laced her fingers with his. "Let's go home," she told him, knowing that as long as they were together she'd found her place in the world.

Griffin watched the light slanting through the window turn from gray to pink as the next morning dawned.

Maggie lay snuggled against him, one arm draped over his chest and her knee pressing into his thigh. As conventional as she was in her waking life, Maggie slept like a crazy woman, constantly tossing and turning with limbs flung in every direction. She even talked in her sleep, mumbling bits of incoherent nonsense throughout the night.

Griffin must have it really bad for this woman because he found even her wild sleeping habits utterly charming. After their first time together yesterday afternoon, they'd made lunch, then played a cutthroat round of Scrabble.

She'd been horrified when he beat her, claiming that a true gentleman would have let her win. He'd countered that a real man knew she had enough brains to beat him without needing to be given the win. So with a gleam in her eye that was exactly what she'd done two more times.

Then he'd carried her up to the bedroom and showed her the exact meaning of her winning word, amorous. They'd spent the evening on the back porch, watching the sun set over the lake as they shared a bottle of wine. He'd told her the ideas he had for the vineyard after talking to Marcus.

Griffin still couldn't quite believe how much he wanted to be involved in Harvest, especially given his determination never to return after that last fight with his father. He wondered what his dad would think of the man he'd become and knew part of what motivated him to stay in Stonecreek was that he still had something to prove.

Too many people remembered the disappointment he'd been to his dad, and he wanted to change that. He wanted to be recognized for how far he'd come in life.

But it was more than that. He'd always loved the land, and there was something satisfying in marking the passage of time by the seasons of the vines.

Maggie was also a big factor in his desire to make their town his permanent home. He smiled as she snuffled, then burrowed more closely against him. He'd told her initially that he wasn't a long-term bet, and she'd still taken him on. Doubt niggled inside his chest, worry that the exact reason she wanted to be with him was because they could have this relationship with no real strings attached.

Now he wanted strings and complications and everything that went with it. He wanted to show her he was there for the long haul. He placed a soft kiss on the top of her head and gingerly got out of bed so as not to wake her.

They weren't expected back in town until tonight, and Griffin was already looking forward to another perfect day with just the two of them.

With the coffee brewing and a pan of bacon sizzling on the stovetop, he walked out onto the back deck, breathing deeply the sultry air of the late-June morning. If only they could stay this way forever, with no issues of family or work to invade this blissful bubble.

A fish jumped in the center of the lake, making him

smile as he thought about Maggie's warrior yell from the previous afternoon. She was so different from the broken, humiliated woman he'd found on the sidewalk that first day back.

He wanted her to always feel as confident as she had in the canoe. The thought that he'd helped her regain her footing filled his chest with a quiet, satisfying pride.

As if he'd summoned her with his thoughts, Maggie appeared at the back door in a white T-shirt and denim shorts. Griffin took one look at her face and a sick pit opened in his stomach.

"What's wrong?"

"We have to go back now," she said, pressing a hand to her chest like she couldn't get a breath.

"Why? What is it?"

"I used the landline to call home this morning to check on Morgan and Ben."

He took a step closer. "Did something—"

"There was a fire," she whispered. "Last night in the tasting room."

Griffin's head swam as he tried to process her words. His world, which minutes earlier had seemed so steady and sure, tilted on its axis, then plummeted to the ground, splintering into a million tiny shards.

"No."

"I'm sorry, Griffin."

The words came to him through a tunnel of denial, hollow and tinny. He was so damn sick of apologies.

"You can use the phone in the living room to call your mom. My dad didn't know how serious the damage was. He heard from—"

"Stop." He held up a hand. How could he call from

here when there was nothing he could do to make it better? He had to see it with his own two eyes. "I need to get back there. Now."

To her credit, Maggie didn't argue or offer platitudes. "I'll grab my keys."

He followed her into the house, only pausing to turn off the stove and unplug the coffeepot before heading toward her car parked out front.

"I'll drive," he told her, and she only hesitated a moment before tossing the keys to him.

The idyllic cabin grew smaller in the rearview mirror, and Griffin had a vile suspicion that his happiness was fading away at the same time.

As soon as they hit the main highway, his phone began to buzz and vibrate, a flurry of missed texts and voice mails coming through.

"We have service," Maggie said, pulling her phone from her purse. "Do you want me to—"

"No." He tightened his grip on the steering wheel. "I want to get home."

Out of the corner of his eye he could see her watching him, fingers squeezed tight around her cell phone. Of course she wanted to find out what had happened at the tasting room, and he knew he sounded crazy. So much anxiety could be alleviated with one quick phone call.

But this unknowing, the teeth-clenching worry, was part of his penance. Whatever caused the fire had happened when he was away. He'd come home for one purpose only—to prove that his dad had been wrong about him. Griffin wanted to make amends for the pain he'd caused his mom all those years ago. To show that he was worthy of being a part of Harvest Vineyards' legacy. Now history was repeating itself, and he hadn't even been there to deal with the disaster.

Had the fire started from a faulty electric wire or something else to do with his work? If he'd been at the barn last night, he might have seen a plume of smoke rise from the tasting room. He might have saved the building the way he hadn't been able to as a teenager.

But he'd been with Maggie, blissfully unaware of anything except his own desires. His father had called him selfish and irresponsible, and maybe those words had been truer than Griffin could stand to admit.

The minutes ticked by as the landscape outside the car went from forest to farmland, the only sound the intermittent chirping from both of their phones. Finally, he pulled into the long, winding drive that led to Harvest.

Heart hammering in his chest and breath coming out in unsteady puffs, he steered the car up the hill toward the tasting room. He felt the weight of Maggie's hand on his arm, but his skin was numb to her touch.

The building came into view, and it was like looking at history come to life all over again. One side of the building remained intact but the southeast corner of the structure was nothing more than blackened boards and a pile of wet ash on the ground.

Several cars were parked in front of the building, and he could see his mother, Marcus and Trevor standing to one side.

He parked and got out of Maggie's car, swallowing back the bile that rose in his throat.

"Was anyone hurt?" he called and felt relief hit him like a tidal wave when his mother shook her head.

"The fire department got it contained within an hour," she reported as he approached.

"Hope you had a great getaway," Trevor said drily. "Once again leaving the rest of us to clean up your mess."

Jana raised a hand before Griffin could respond. "Don't do that, Trevor. This isn't Griffin's mess. The fire would have happened whether he'd been here or not."

Trevor didn't look convinced, and Griffin couldn't blame him. "What caused it?"

Marcus stepped forward so that he was standing between Griffin and Trevor. "They think it was a candle that got knocked over."

"We don't have candles in there," Griffin said. "It's a construction site."

"Someone was trespassing last night," Trevor reported, and Griffin frowned as his brother shifted to look at Maggie. "One of the neighbors saw a red Jeep racing away from the property when he let his dog out before bed. Mom saw the flames just after eleven."

"You think Morgan had something to do with this?" Maggie's voice was high and tight. "That's a bold accusation, Trevor."

"She was here yesterday." Jana wrapped her arms tight around her middle. "I'm sorry, Maggie, but I heard her fighting with the Maren boy when I was taking my evening walk."

"Cole wanted some extra hours so I knew he was here." Griffin moved closer to the fire-ravaged building, reached out to run his fingers over the charred wood.

He glanced back to see his mother nodding. "They

were out here. I didn't think much of it until Fred mentioned the Jeep."

"Morgan didn't cause the fire," Maggie said, stalking forward. "You can't accuse her of this without proof."

"No one's accusing your sister," Marcus said gently.

"But it's suspicious," Trevor added.

"Why would she do this?" Maggie demanded. Griffin turned as she jabbed a finger at Trevor. "You don't want this tasting room to open. I know you want to see your new grand fancy building take its place. Maybe you're trying to frame Morgan."

"You think I want to start a fire on this property?" Trevor threw up his hands. "I'm going to have enough of a PR nightmare dealing with questions about smoke taint after this. What if the fire had spread to the vines? It would have been devastating." He leveled a look at Maggie. "But not to your family."

"Trevor." Marcus's voice was firm. "This isn't helping. Placing blame prematurely isn't going to do any good."

"Whatever." Trevor shook his head. "I've got phone calls to return. We all know who in this community benefits most by hurting Harvest."

He stalked off down the sloping hill toward the main office on the other side of the open courtyard.

Griffin wanted to yell or hit something or walk away. *Run away.* Life had been easier when he wasn't emotionally involved. Right now he couldn't figure out what to feel. Anger...regret...guilt. He'd spent years trying to convince himself he wanted nothing to do with the family business after his father kicked him out. Now he was back but his second chance seemed doomed, much like the happiness he thought he'd found.

Maggie stood in stunned silence as she watched Trevor walk away. Marcus gave her an apologetic smile while Jana seemed to deliberately avoid eye contact.

They couldn't truly believe Morgan had anything to do with the fire? And certainly not that it was some sort of larger scheme to undermine their family business.

Griffin would never stand for that.

Would he?

"We'll rebuild," Jana said gently, putting a hand on Griffin's broad shoulder. He didn't move or react; he just continued to stare at the fire-ravaged building in front of him.

Jana gave him a short hug, then turned and joined Marcus at the edge of the gravel drive. It was clear they were giving Maggie and Griffin a bit of privacy. Maggie only wished she knew how to make this better.

She remembered the first fire at the tasting room. She'd driven her grandmother out here to survey the damage. Harvest had been a fledgling business at that point, and Dave Stone had looked as shell-shocked as Griffin did now when he'd met them on this very same hill.

That was the moment she'd learned that Griffin had left town. It had been a shock, and Dave's voice sounded hollow as he spoke of his careless, reckless son and the damage he'd caused.

Maggie knew how much it meant to Griffin to rebuild this part of his family's property. She walked toward him, aching to offer whatever comfort she could.

"You should go," he said, stepping away as if he couldn't stand to have her too close.

"I want to help," Maggie said, "both as the mayor and as your friend. I know everyone is upset and angry, but you can't possibly believe my family had anything to do with this."

"This isn't about you," he said, his tone biting.

She swallowed, shocked at the insinuation of his words. "I know, Griffin. But it's not about Morgan, either."

"Your sister is a spoiled, self-centered kid." He turned, and the anger in the depths of his eyes felt like poison seeping through her veins—destroying her from the inside out. "I should know because I was one."

"That doesn't mean—"

"You Spencers like to believe you're above everyone else in this town, that you hold some sort of exalted status because of your last name."

"You're not being fair," Maggie insisted. Where was the man who had held her so tenderly through the night? Who laughed at her silly jokes and made her feel like she could accomplish anything? "If Morgan was involved, we'll make it right."

"You can't," he said quietly, then turned and walked away.

Maggie stood there for several moments, too stunned to move. Everything she'd thought they meant to each other was gone. She realized her dreams were castles built from sand, easily toppled by the smallest wave.

"Give him time," Marcus said from behind her.

"Why?" she asked, a tremble in her voice.

"The fire is messing with his head. It puts him back

to where he was ten years ago, and that was a bad time for the whole family. Even if Morgan had something to do with that candle, we all know it was an accident."

"Griffin doesn't seem to," she muttered. "The things he said...that he believes about us."

"He's angry and emotional."

"It's not an excuse." She took a deep breath and squared her shoulders. "I need to talk to my sister. Would you call Cole to get his side of the story?"

Marcus nodded. "We'll figure it out, Maggie."

She swallowed back the tears rising in her throat and walked to her car, wondering if her life would ever feel normal again.

Chapter Fifteen

"They're going to hate me forever," Morgan said from the back seat of their father's Volvo station wagon later that evening.

"They won't hate you," Maggie said, although her stomach knotted in anticipation of the meeting with the Stones.

She'd returned home earlier, numb from the barrage of Griffin's words to find Morgan concerned about the fire at the winery but unaware she'd had any part in it.

Maggie had sat down with Morgan and their dad, explaining what she knew about the circumstances of the blaze. Her sister's face immediately lost all of its color as she began to hyperventilate, realizing that her careless actions had caused the blaze.

When Maggie finally got Morgan calm enough to speak coherently, the girl explained that she had a crush on Cole and had gone to the winery knowing he was working late that evening. She'd set up a romantic tableau in the empty building, complete with candles, a blanket and a bottle of wine she'd stolen from the rack in the kitchen.

It had taken a bit of coaxing to keep Jim Spencer from getting totally sidetracked by the idea that his teenage daughter had wanted to seduce a boy. Maggie managed to pull from Morgan that Cole had rebuffed her advances, leading to a huge argument. Morgan claimed she'd thrown everything she'd brought into her backpack and driven away, but admitted that she might have left behind a candle in her hurry to get away.

Maggie had been unable to reach Jana or Griffin to explain the situation, so they were driving out to the vineyard so Morgan could apologize in person and Jim could work out the details of making restitution for the damages.

If they handled this privately, Maggie hoped they could avoid getting law enforcement involved. But based on Griffin's anger earlier, she wasn't sure what might happen.

Her father parked in front of Jana's house and Maggie put an arm around Morgan's waist as they walked up the front porch steps as somber as a funeral procession.

Jim knocked and a minute later Jana appeared at the door.

"Jim," she whispered like she'd just seen a ghost.

"Hello, Jana." Maggie glanced sharply at her father, something in his tone making her think there was more to his greeting than the two simple words.

He ran a hand over his clean-shaven jaw. "I know

this is a difficult time," he said slowly, "and we wouldn't be here if it wasn't important."

She looked from him to Maggie and then Morgan, the corners of her mouth dipping slightly. "Come in."

Maggie had been in the Stone family home countless times, but today she took in the expensive furnishings, the framed black-and-white photos, everything neat as a pin and so different from her cozy, cluttered family home.

"Have a seat," Jana offered, gesturing to the damask-covered sofa and two coordinating side chairs arranged in the living room.

Maggie's father took a seat on the far side of the couch, and Maggie ushered Morgan next to him before sitting. She tugged on her sister's hand when Morgan continued to stand, but the girl ignored her.

Jana clasped her hands in front of her stomach, looking as formal as the decor. "May I get anyone a glass of wat—"

"I'm so sorry," Morgan blurted, then covered her mouth with a hand as her shoulders shook uncontrollably. "It was an accident. The candle… I didn't mean…"

"It's all right, dear," Jana said gently, tension slipping from her petite frame. She came forward and reached a hand out to pat Morgan's arm. "Cole explained everything. We know what he did."

Maggie straightened as her sister went perfectly still. "Cole didn't do anything," Morgan whispered.

"What did he tell you, Jana?" Maggie asked.

Jana closed her eyes, dragged in what looked to be a calming breath, then opened her eyes again. "He said he invited you to the property and when you weren't receptive to his advances, he got angry. I believe he didn't realize he'd knocked over the candle after your argument." She flashed a wistful smile. "I was young once so I remember how emotions can sometimes get the best of us."

"That isn't how it happened." Morgan looked between Maggie and their father, who stood and paced to the window, massaging a hand over the back of his neck. "I came out here on my own."

"Are you protecting him, Morgan?" Jim demanded, turning around and gripping the back of the tufted side chair. "Did that boy try to take advantage of you?"

"No," Morgan insisted. "Maggie, you know Cole. He isn't like that."

"Don't worry," Jana assured them. "We're not going to press charges. Griffin..." Her voice trailed off and she sighed and then continued, "Griffin appreciates his honesty. Obviously, this isn't the first time teenage emotions have had devastating repercussions on our vineyard."

"I left the candle burning," Morgan said, her voice rising. "I got mad and stormed off and forgot it. Cole didn't do anything."

"He's going to work to pay off the cost of the repairs," Jana continued as if Morgan hadn't spoken. "It might take a while, but Griffin had no reservations about giving him a second chance."

"Maggie." Morgan turned, disbelief and guilt warring in her eyes. "You can't let him take the blame for this."

Dumbfounded at the boy's sacrifice, Maggie turned to Jana, who held up a hand. "He warned us Morgan would defend him this way." Her smile was gentle. "You've raised a good girl, Jim. You should be proud."

"No," Morgan whispered. "Dad, no."

"I'll pay for the reconstruction," Maggie's father said, stepping around the chair, closer to Jana. "I don't know what happened here last night, but that boy shouldn't have to bear the responsibility of it."

Jana's eyes widened. "But he said—"

"I know what Cole told you, and I know what Morgan explained to us. But only the two of them know the truth."

"Dad," Morgan said, her voice a low whine. "I'm not lying. I promise."

"Teenage promises," he murmured, never taking his eyes off Jana. "You and I both know how well those can be trusted."

Maggie frowned as Jana drew in a sharp breath. What did she not understand about her father's history with Griffin's mother?

"I'll have Griffin contact you once he has figures on what it will take to fix the damage. I can't guarantee Cole will appreciate your generosity…"

"He doesn't need to. They both have some responsibility in this. I'll talk to Griffin about how Morgan can do her part."

"Fine."

They stared at each other for several seconds, and Maggie wished she could see her father's face. When he finally turned, his gaze was unreadable.

"Let's go," he said and Maggie wondered where her absentminded father had gone. In his place stood a man who looked ready to go to war for or against his younger daughter. Maggie couldn't quite decide which.

Morgan looked like she wanted to argue, but Maggie took her hand and led her from the room.

As soon as they were out of the house, Morgan wrenched away from her grasp. "This isn't fair."

"No more from you," Jim said. "You *will* turn this around, Morgan. You've been given a chance here."

"What about Cole?"

Their father narrowed his eyes. "That boy is not my responsibility."

"Dad," Maggie and Morgan said at once.

Jim blew out a long breath. "Fine. I'll make sure Griffin understands that Cole is trying to take the blame for something he didn't do. I won't let anything bad happen to him."

With a soft cry, Morgan threw her arms around their father's waist and burrowed into his chest. "Thanks, Daddy," she whispered.

Maggie met his gaze and nodded, her nerves settling at the knowledge that one section of her life was slowly getting back on track.

It was nearly midnight before she made it back down to the cabin to pack up from earlier. Her father had suggested she wait until the following day, but Maggie knew she wouldn't sleep tonight and so welcomed the distraction.

Her heart stuttered as her headlights picked up the outline of Griffin's Land Cruiser already parked in the driveway.

The lights were on in the cabin, and she could see him in the kitchen, moving back and forth from the refrigerator to the counter. She hadn't bothered to lock the door when they'd rushed out this morning.

She wanted to put the car into Reverse, to speed away and avoid the confrontation she knew was inevitable. But this was her mess to clean up as much as his, so she parked and walked up the steps to the front door, trying to keep her heartbeat steady.

He glanced up as she entered the kitchen.

"I can take care of this," she said, wishing he would leave without speaking.

"I made you hurry out this morning." He picked up a pan from the drainer next to the sink and began to wipe it dry. "It's the least I can do."

She crossed her arms over her chest, hating the implication of his words. "You didn't make me do anything."

One side of his mouth curved. "Good to know."

"I'm sorry about the tasting room," she said quietly, moving forward to put the rest of the supplies into the cardboard box he'd set on the counter.

"We'll rebuild."

"My dad and I brought Morgan over to talk to your mom today." Maggie shouldn't have brought her sister into the conversation. There was enough tension between Griffin and her without adding more. But she had to address it.

He inclined his head. "Your dad left me a message."

She waited for him to say more.

"It wasn't Cole's fault," she whispered when he remained silent.

"I know."

"But Morgan isn't all of the things you accused her of being. My family doesn't have it out for yours that way."

He shrugged. "If you say so."

"Do you really believe that?"

"I don't know what to believe at this point," he admitted.

"Me, neither," she agreed. "It's all so complicated."

"Complicated isn't really my thing."

"I understand."

"Do you?"

"No, but I get what you're telling me. You can't be with me."

"I want to."

"Sure." It felt like a boot was stomping across her chest.

"I'm sorry," he whispered and then closed his eyes. "Damn, I hate apologies."

"I need you to leave," she said.

"Maggie."

"Please, Griffin." She hated that her voice broke on his name. "Please," she repeated, looking down at the floor, unable to watch him walk away.

Listening to his footsteps and then the front door opening and closing was bad enough. She gripped the edge of the counter, willing herself to stay standing as tears poured down her cheeks. This moment would not break her. She'd been through too much to be felled by an aching heart now.

But she wouldn't force back the tears. She needed to feel everything if she had any chance of moving forward. She walked through the cabin, packing her belongings and loading them into her car. Griffin had packed his stuff and done most of the cleaning before she arrived, so once her bags were in the trunk, she turned off the lights, locked the front door and headed back home.

As she entered her father's darkened house, a light flipped on in the living room, revealing her dad in the big leather recliner that had been his official chair since she was a girl.

"You doing okay?" he asked gently.

"No." She dropped her backpack to the hardwood floor. "Griffin was at the cabin."

"Things didn't go well, I take it?"

She leaned against the door frame. "Spencers and Stones aren't meant to mix."

"I could have told you that," he said with a quiet chuckle.

"Why didn't you?"

He gave an apologetic shake of his head. "I never thought you needed my advice. You were always so sure of yourself, Maggie. You and your grandmother never seemed to have doubts about anything."

"I have plenty of doubts," she admitted, "and Grammy is at the heart of most of them."

"I'm a lousy father," Jim said with a sigh.

"You did good today."

"Thanks, girl. But I want to do good for you, too."

"Was I elected mayor only because of Grammy?" she asked.

Her father smiled. "No, despite what your grandmother would have you believe."

"I want to lead this town, all of it."

"You can," he assured her.

"But if I go against Grammy, will it cost me the election?"

"I hope not. I guarantee you've got my vote."

"Thanks, Dad," she whispered and smiled. One way

or another, she'd find a way to keep going. Maggie's heart might be splintered, but she refused to break.

The life she'd created was too precious to give up on it now.

* * * * *

Can Maggie and Griffin settle their families' feud?
Will Maggie's mayoral dreams come to fruition?
Find out in

Second Chance in Stonecreek

Book 2 of the Maggie & Griffin trilogy,
available October 2018 wherever
Harlequin Special Edition books
and ebooks are sold!

COMING NEXT MONTH FROM

H HARLEQUIN®

SPECIAL EDITION

Available September 18, 2018

#2647 UNMASKING THE MAVERICK
Montana Mavericks: The Lonelyhearts Ranch • by Teresa Southwick
Rugged former marine Brendan Tanner recently moved to Rust Creek
Falls and is shocked by the sparks that fly between him and Fiona O'Reilly.
They're both gun-shy when it comes to love, but maybe Fiona will succeed in
unmasking this maverick's heart!

#2648 ALMOST A BRAVO
The Bravos of Valentine Bay • by Christine Rimmer
Aislinn Bravo just found out she was switched at birth—and to fulfill her
biological father's will, she must marry Jaxon Winters. She thought she had
buried any feelings for Jaxon long ago, but when they're forced to spend three
months as husband and wife, those feelings come roaring back to the surface.

#2649 SECOND CHANCE IN STONE CREEK
Maggie & Griffin • by Michelle Major
No matter how much mayor Maggie Spencer avoids bad boy Griffin Stone,
there's only so far to go in Stonecreek. Only so long she can deny an
undeniable attraction. Their families are feuding, the gossip is threatening
her reelection, but nothing can keep her away...

#2650 THE RANCHER'S CHRISTMAS PROMISE
Return to the Double C • by Allison Leigh
Ryder Wilson is determined to make a home for the baby his late estranged
wife left on a stranger's doorstep. Local lawyer Greer Templeton is there to
help. It's enough to make Ryder propose a marriage of convenience. But
does love factor into his Christmas promise?

#2651 THE TEXAS COWBOY'S QUADRUPLETS
Texas Legends: The McCabes • by Cathy Gillen Thacker
Mitzi Martin is desperate to save her newly inherited business—while raising
infant quadruplets! Chase McCabe only wants to help but their previous
broken engagement makes it difficult to convince Mitzi he's sincere. Can he
save her business and convince Mitzi to give him another chance?

#2652 THE CAPTAINS' VEGAS VOWS
American Heroes • by Caro Carson
An impromptu Vegas wedding lands two army captains in married quarters
while they wait for the ninety-day waiting period required to get a divorce.
She thinks she's not cut out for marriage and he doesn't believe in love. Will
ninety days be enough to find their happily-ever-after?

**YOU CAN FIND MORE INFORMATION ON UPCOMING HARLEQUIN® TITLES,
FREE EXCERPTS AND MORE AT WWW.HARLEQUIN.COM.**

HSECNM0918

"So, the boot is finally on the other foot."

Mitzy Martin stared at the indomitable CEO standing on
the other side of her front door, looking more rancher than
businessman in nice-fitting jeans, boots and a tan Western
shirt. Ignoring the skittering of her heart, she heaved a sigh
to convey just how unwelcome he was. "What's your point,
cowboy?"

Mischief gleaming in his smoky-blue eyes, Chase looked
her up and down in a way that made her insides flutter. "Just
that you've been a social worker in Laramie County for
what…ten years now?"

Electricity sparked between them with all the danger of
a downed power line. "Eleven," Mitzy corrected. And it had
been slightly longer than that. Since she'd abruptly ended
their engagement…

"My guess is, very few people are happy to see you
coming up their front walk. Now you seem to be feeling
that," he continued with an ornery grin, "seeing *me* at your
door."

Mitzy drew a breath, ignoring the considerable physical
awareness that never failed to materialize between them.

She gave him a long, level look to show him he was *not* going to get to her. Even if his square jaw and chiseled features, sandy-brown hair and incredibly buff physique were permanently imprinted on her brain. She smiled sweetly. "Well, when people get to know me and realize I'm there to help, they usually become quite warm and friendly."

He surveyed her pleasantly. "That's exactly what I hope will happen between you and me. Now that we're older and wiser, that is."

Mitzy glared. She and Chase had crashed and burned once—spectacularly. There was no way she was doing it again.

He stepped closer, inundating her with his wildly intoxicating scent. "Mitzy, come on. You've been ducking my calls for weeks now."

So what? "I know it's hard for a carefree bachelor like you to understand, but I've been 'a little busy' since giving birth to quadruplets."

He shrugged. "Word around town is you've had *plenty* of volunteer help. Plus the high-end nannies your mother sent from Dallas."

Mitzy groaned and clapped a hand across her forehead.

"Didn't work out?"

"No," she bit out. "Just like this lobbying effort on your part won't work, either."

"Look, I know you'd rather not do business with me," he said, even more gently. "But at least hear me out."

Don't miss
The Texas Cowboy's Quadruplets
by Cathy Gillen Thacker.

Available October 2018 wherever
Harlequin® Special Edition *books and ebooks are sold.*

www.Harlequin.com

⊞HARLEQUIN®

SPECIAL EDITION

Life, Love and Family

COMING NEXT MONTH!

Cathy Gillen Thacker
debuts her heartfelt series
Texas Legends: The McCabes
in **Harlequin Special Edition**.

Don't miss
THE TEXAS COWBOY'S QUADRUPLETS
Available October 2018

Read the first two books in the
Texas Legends: The McCabes series
from Harlequin Western Romance:
The Texas Cowboy's Baby Rescue
The Texas Cowboy's Triplets